LYNDON PEARSON

THE
BIRDS
IN MY HEAD
FINALLY
LEARNED TO
SING

outskirts
press

Outskirts Press, Inc.
http://www.outskirtspress.com

ISBN: 978-1-9772-4232-7

Cover Photo 2021 Gary Cheadle. All rights reserved - used with permission.

Author Photo 2021 @ty_pleas. All rights reserved - used by permission.

Outskirts Press and the "OP" logo are trademarks belonging to Outskirts Press, Inc.

PRINTED IN THE UNITED STATES OF AMERICA

Acknowledgements

I would like to thank God for revealing my purpose in life to help others heal their heart through the gift of writing. Thank you to my mother Marlin Pearson for insisting that I include prayer and more prayer with all the research, books and alternative medicine that I "discovered" over the years during the writing of this book.

Thank you to Beverly Gilbert for your encouragement, your spiritual gift of listening and for entering my life at the exact moment when I needed a friend. Joseph Jordan, you were the secret weapon I needed to complete this project. You came along exactly when the timing was right (look at God). Thank you for your insight and willingness to help me think beyond the walls of the church to reach this generation through ministry.

Thank you to Mrs. Beryl Daley, Mrs. Emma Faust, Mrs. Laura Turnbull and countless others that held my sister and my mother up in prayer as we searched for answers.

Thank you God for the Greystone Psychiatric Hospital and staff of unit F-2. Nurse Velma, you are an angel. My sister was more than just a patient at Greystone Hospital under your compassionate care. You touched her life and changed mine in the process.

Thank you to my editors: Addriene Rhodes, Nickoleta Lytras and Breanna Armand. You made the crazy story in my mind make sense. Thank you to my graphic artist, Gary Cheadle, for bringing my book cover design out of my head. I would like to thank @ty_pleas for capturing my "essence" in your book photo. Thank you to the staff of Outskirts Publishing for providing the platform for me to share my story.

Thank you to my lifelong (since college) friends, Mark & Michelle Cooper and Patrick & Carla Minor for your continued support.

Aunt Ruth & Uncle Bud…you are my rock and I love you.

I would also like to thank my friends and social media followers for keeping me covered and lifted in prayer as I allowed this awesome story of love throughout life's storms to unfold.

God bless…

Author's Note

Mental illness is no laughing matter.

When the symptoms show up on your doorstep and it's your immediate family member or loved ones that are affected, the one thing
I have found to make it through the journey and the pain is laughter. Find friends that will support you, because you will need their
strength for the journey. Also, surround yourself with people that will
allow you to cry along the way.

Remember, supporting your loved ones living with mental illness is
one of life's greatest gifts. Most importantly, take time to laugh.

Lyndon "Len" Pearson

For help with mental illness, please contact
(NAMI) National Alliance on Mental Illness
800-950-NAMI (6264).
website: nami.org

I have heard your prayer;
I have seen your tears.
Behold, I will heal you.
II Kings 20:5

Table of Contents

CHAPTER 1
Building A Nest

Staring out the window seemed to be more of an acquired habit than anything else as Sunshine found herself at the windowsill of her dorm room for hours at a time. Since Sunshine had entered her freshman year of college, nothing seemed to captivate her attention more than the seat at her dorm window. The window in her room was not anything spectacular other than it offered the only sensible escape, besides the front door, in case of an emergency. Either out of pure boredom or perhaps due to the beauty of the tranquil campus setting, Sunshine found herself spending a significant amount of time in her daily schedule to sit at her window seat.

Upon meeting her new roommate with the unusual name of Belle, Sunshine quickly noticed that she was always smiling, laughing and enjoying life. Although Belle was from Los Angeles, California, and enjoyed mostly year-round great weather, Sunshine still felt like the luckiest girl in the world. For some strange reason, she could not figure out why she felt so lucky, even as she looked at her roommate with the side-eye. While Belle meticulously unpacked her bags during the orientation weekend when all new students arrived on campus, Sunshine fell onto her bed and let out a sigh of relief as she saw some of the beautiful designer blouses and fancy jeans that her roommate pulled from her suitcases. *Thank God,* Sunshine breathed in relief, *at least my biggest fear of having a roommate with only two changes of clothes will not happen.*

To avoid facing the possibility of having to share her clothes, Sunshine had spent practically the whole summer buying extra outfits, undergarments and toiletries for her yet to be determined roommate. Growing up without a sister, Sunshine had no experience on how to share her clothes with another female and had no intention to start just because she was heading off to college.

With no look of worry on her face Belle continued to unpack, silently assuring Sunshine with each garment she hung in the closet with the tag still visible that borrowing clothes would not be their issue. Still, Sunshine struggled to figure out why in the world she felt so happy. As she tore her eyes away from the elegant black Donna Karan pant-suit that Belle pulled out of her seemingly magic suitcase, Sunshine thought she had finally stumbled on the reason for her happiness. She continued her gaze out of her dormitory window of Peterson Hall and past all the fears and unknowns of freshman life. Sunshine could not believe that her joy seemed to be coming from her gaze that was transfixed outside of her window. The big red brick dormitory was the designated residence for all incoming freshman women and faced the northeast corner of the campus, overlooking the luscious farmland tucked off behind the school. To the naked eye, anyone who decided to glance out the window would quickly surmise that there was not much to look at other than a whole lotta grass and a few cows.

But for Sunshine, the angle and picturesque view from her dormitory window brought back a surge of warm memories and somehow made everything that she was about to face as a college student seem more bearable. Ironically, it was not that long ago that Sunshine had labored for months at the windowsill of her own house waiting for her big brother, Lil Son, to come around the corner fresh from his first semester at college. When her brother initially left, he called home almost every weekend, even if most of the time the underlying reason was a desperate plea for money. Sunshine relished each phone call and listened intently to his elaborate stories about college life and his perceived new-found freedom.

During the first couple of weeks of his absence, the days rolled by ever so slowly as Sunshine anticipated her brother would soon bend the corner for a surprise visit home. The reality was that it turned out to be just a smidge shy of four months before Lil Son came home during the Christmas break for his first visit from college. To Sunshine, the time and distance apart from her best friend seemed more like an eternity. Now, some ten years later, Sunshine felt like the little girl inside had come full circle in her young life because she was now about to embark on her very own college experience.

With all her might, Sunshine held tightly to those fleeting memories of sitting at the windowsill waving goodbye to her brother and best friend in the entire world. For some lucky explosion, she felt blessed to have the most breathtaking window seat to take in the amazing view of her journey into young adult life.

On a personal level, there was a great amount of significance in the fact that this extremely shy little girl landed at this particular university in the middle of the northern section of Alabama. For no other reason than the fact that her older brother was the famous music producer and Grammy award winner who had attended this very school just ten years earlier, Sunshine felt compelled to follow in her brother's footprints. On campus, as she walked the hallowed grounds, she would hear the soft banter from her fellow students. They whispered in hushed voices, "That's the baby sister of Lil Son, the famous music producer." Excitedly, they continued sharing the news: "He's the person who discovered Raelyn, the Gem of the South and the heir apparent to the legendary queen of gospel Mahalia Jackson." Although they were no longer an item or making music together, their smash hit single, "My Friend," stayed on the Top 20 Billboard charts for thirty-two weeks and made the two of them household names.

It was kinda weird the first couple times that it happened, but as the days rolled by during the first semester of the school year, all the whisperings that Sunshine perceived as she walked around campus or simply entered a room were taking their toll. *After all,* Sunshine thought to herself, *I'm just a freshman. I don't need the headache.* Just like her brother had experienced a ground swell of local celebrity as word spread around campus about his musical genius, it just made sense that a mere decade later the college community would still be enamored with Lil Son's musical gift. The fact that his sister had chosen the same college automatically made her a minor local celebrity by pure coincidence or default, depending on the level of admiration or jealousy.

The toll of being a freshman in college on any campus in the country is usually pretty inundating for countless students each year, but Sunshine felt like no one understood the pressure she was under as she walked around her new home away from home. For the most part, she knew young people viewed college through the lens of an opportunity to escape their childhood memories or as a platform to help jumpstart what their future may hold. But not Sunshine. With every look or smile that she encountered, college in her mind was fast becoming a tightening noose around her neck, and her initial swell of hope and happiness was slowly being replaced by tension and stress that she couldn't seem to shake.

Somehow Sunshine hadn't realized the length and breadth of her own celebrity until the president of the college expressed his elation that she had chosen her brother's alma mater and decided to make her stand up during the candlelight orientation service to acknowledge the occasion. Not one day had passed since the new student convocation and the unannounced spotlight placed on her by the president made Sunshine Black feel like she could not explore the campus as a regular student. Everywhere she went, she was known and recognized as the girl that happened to be the baby sister of Lil Son.

The simple act by the president of the school to welcome the sister of arguably the most famous alumnus brought even more un-solicited spotlight to Sunshine's situation. The esteemed *Rolling Stone* magazine had courageously labeled Lil Son's entry into the gospel music industry as the "greatest musical milestone of the decade."

But none of this extra limelight and red carpet treatment that so many people desired was appealing to Sunshine. "It could all disap-pear today," she whispered softly to herself as she took her seat and the applause died down in the waning minutes of the convocation. *All I want to do is be by myself*, Sunshine mused, as she looked up and glanced over the faces of her fellow freshmen and the unapolo-getic glow in their eyes. It seemed as if the sparkle and extra glow were the collective realization that they must get to know the newly-crowned most popular girl on campus.

Sunshine had come to recognize the familiar twinkle of the eyes and the sudden effort to be nice to her once people found out exactly who she was related to in the music business. From as far back as she could remember, sometime around the third grade when her brother's first hit single "My Friend" rapidly climbed the music charts, people started treating Sunshine as if she were something special. With each milestone and award ceremony in her brother's fabulous life, espe-cially the televised appearances on The Babbie Mason Show and the pinnacle of gospel music, The Stellar Awards, the changes in peo-ple's behavior grew increasingly bizarre. As high school finally rolled around, Sunshine found it more convenient to divide up her whole life into two parts: life as she knew it before her brother left for college and life after her brother received two Grammys as a new artist. On that amazing night, he received two of the most coveted awards of the night, the Producer of the Year and Song of the Year Award.

Lil Son's wins in both categories were long shots at best, and most in the industry had to scramble after the show to get in touch with his people for a hot song or collabo before his prices quadrupled. Soon after "the show," as the epic Grammy win was categorized to separate it from all the other award shows, Sunshine's fellow classmates started helping her with her homework and sharing their lunch items. But the most startling addition since the spectacular night was all the attention from the boys at school, even the ones who could talk to any girl they wanted. To her surprise, the cute guys started having eyes for her, and Sunshine knew it because she would look up from her desk and catch them staring and unable to look away.

Although boys were on her radar and bucket list of things to explore, Sunshine found it hard to think about anything else in those early weeks other than the fact that each day apart seemed to cast her further and further from her brother and best friend. As far back as she could remember, Sunshine and her brother had always been very close. Despite the ten-year difference in their ages, Sunshine felt that no one knew her innermost thoughts better than her big brother. He was her everything and when he left home to embark on this new milestone called college, it was the final straw her young mind seemed to use to tear them apart. Nothing was able to shake their bond and love for one another except for that distant dream that he had described as fame.

"My brother is super talented without a doubt," Sunshine chuckled out loud, "but somehow along the way I became collateral damage in his quest for fame and fortune." Allowing herself a moment to reflect over the last couple of days since school started, Sunshine thought, *I can't believe I haven't heard from him since I left home in the middle of August for my own college experience. Not one single email, tweet or phone call since the start of my college journey. Who would treat their best friend like that?* "College is supposed to be the biggest milestone in my life," Sunshine remarked out loud as she sat alone eating her lunch, "and I must read the blogs to find out what in the world my famous brother is doing."

Literally.

Sitting in the corner of the cafeteria picking at her salad while trying to be invisible, Sunshine suddenly realized how much she missed her best friend. "If only Lil Son were here to listen to me, perhaps I wouldn't feel so alone on this beautiful campus," Sunshine whispered. Slowly she raised her head and looked up to find her roommate, Belle, staring at her with the crazy eye. "Best friend, how many times do I need to ask, can I sit here?" Without waiting on Sunshine's slow response and seeing three empty chairs, Belle plopped down, looking exhausted from a full day of college life.

Without a clue as to what was bothering her roommate, Belle asked, "Why are you acting so weird? It's like something is taking over your mind." Not knowing how to respond to such a bizarre question, Sunshine decided to blow it off as overly invasive and inappropriate and react in a manner which was in her comfort zone.

She decided to run.

Running was a sudden and effective learned behavior that Sunshine had found to be an immediate bandage to any situation that felt uncomfortable. When her brother left for college and the feelings of abandonment crept into her thought pattern, Sunshine ultimately ran to the safety and serenity of her bedroom window seat.

Now, without saying another word, she stood up, grabbed her books and cell phone and ran out of the cafeteria. She hurriedly ran past Carter Hall, rushing past the students waving to her near the student center, straight to her dorm room and the solitude of her window.

Finally. Home sweet home!

Nothing seemed to bring as much comfort and escape from the world as the privacy of her dorm room and the tranquility of her windowsill. Completely out of breath from her track race across campus, Sunshine finally found herself alone in the solitude of her dorm room. Within fifteen feet from her doorknob stood her dorm window and the serenity of her very own secret garden that her eyes longed all day to gaze upon.

While she drank some water to cool off and wait for her heart rate to slow down, her eyes suddenly became fixated on movement going on near her window. Walking cautiously closer to investigate who would have the impertinence to invade her space, Sunshine found a lone bird, perhaps a sparrow, she imagined, perched on her windowsill. *What in the world would a bird be doing way up here on the third floor of my dormitory building and near my secret place of rest,* Sunshine thought to herself.

"Would you please leave, Mr. Bird. I want to be alone!" she exclaimed.

Sunshine yelled and simultaneously flailed her arms at the poor bird as she hurried to sink into the pillows that she gathered around her small frame on the bed for her moment of serenity near her windowsill. Inexplicably, the sparrow had no idea that Sunshine needed a moment alone or was having anything other than a blessed day. The poor little bird, impervious to Sunshine's presence, continued to occupy his time with his unannounced chirping noises and nest building. With her roommate securely nestled in the cafeteria eating supper minus her former dinner companion, Sunshine felt safe coming out of her comfort zone to communicate with the lone bird. With somewhat reckless abandon, she wished and hoped over and over that the poor bird would just decide to fly away. But when the uninvited guest failed to read her thoughts, Sunshine reverted into her secret feelings until they unexpectedly bubbled over into a verbal outrage.

"Go away, Mr. Bird," she noisily shouted.

With her hands flapping wildly in the air for several minutes as if the bird understood sign language, it soon became clear to Sunshine that the bird had chosen the same exact windowsill for his place of comfort and rest. Upon grasping that the bird was steadfast in his land grab as a member of the animal kingdom, Sunshine quickly realized that all her antics of bird shooing were going to be in vain and very exhausting at best.

Instead, Sunshine transferred her attention from her strenuous arm waving and became enamored with the diligence and fortitude that the sparrow was using to build his nest. Nothing else mattered for the next hour as Sunshine fixed her eyes on the intense urgency which the sparrow manifested to gather his sticks and leaves to build his home. Fascinated by the nest building of the little sparrow, Sunshine had no idea that this was more than just an invasion of her quiet time at her windowsill.

Little did she know that the chirping noises that the sparrow spewed out of his beak was more than just bird gibberish and some-how he would soon reveal his true purpose to her young life.

CHAPTER 2
Can I Stay Here?

The noise was growing louder and it was becoming increasingly hard for Belle to stay in the REM phase of sleep as she rolled over in bed. "This is ridiculous," she scoffed. Reluctantly, she forced open one eye and squinted with the other as the noise of a bed moving across the floor matched the silhouette of a person caught in the act.

"Roommate, what on earth are you doing up so early? Why are you making so much noise?" Belle yelled toward the scratching noise.

Feeling slightly embarrassed for waking her roommate at the crack of dawn, Sunshine placed her index finger over her lips as a silent promise to be quiet. And with just two more heaves of her shoulder against the wooden bedpost, coupled with the awkward screeching of furniture being scraped across the floor, Sunshine let out a sigh of relief that her bed was now squarely up against the windowsill. From her first observation some five days ago when Mr. Bird, as she named her new friend, came storming into her life, Sunshine could not get enough of her unsolicited guest. And now with her bed firmly against the only window in the room, Sunshine felt that she could devote all her spare time to her very entertaining, yet unplanned, new friend.

But somehow Sunshine had forgotten to calculate the amount of time her roommate would demand in conversation simply because they shared the same college dorm room. For the first couple of nights, Belle managed to keep her roommate captivated, telling stories about growing up in the city of Los Angeles as a preacher's kid and all the celebrities she would bump into in the town of make-believe and fantasy. Nonetheless, by the second week of school, her words eventually lost all their worldly luster and fascination and mostly fell short of reaching Sunshine's distant ear. With the concentration of the biblical David preparing to send a rock into the forehead of Goliath, Sunshine tried her best to pay attention to Belle. But for some strange reason Sunshine at times didn't feel like she was really in the same dorm room watching her roommate's mouth open and close. In her mind, she felt like a random person or object was sitting inside her head shouting massive amounts of illogical thoughts back at her. From Belle's mouth full of titillating Hollywood information to Sunshine's unconcerned eardrum, it all soon started to sound like blah blah blah and more blah. In fact, nothing seemed to enter Sunshine's mindfulness and consume space like the action taking place outside her window, which was absolutely taking her breath away.

Over the course of several days since seeing his new friend at the windowsill, Mr. Bird would fly back and forth countless times with a twig or a leaf inside his beak as he prepared his new home for his family. Sunshine had never seen any creature build their home from scratch and soon became enthralled with the entire nest building process.

With the newness of college life wearing off, Sunshine was finally settling into the day to day hum of school existence. There were tons of classes, reports, rehearsals and activities pulling at this "fresh meat" freshman for a piece of her twenty-four-hour daily cycle. But nothing seemed to balance out her day like the comfort of her front row seat at her window.

No one told me that college was going to be so exhausting, Sunshine thought to herself. The weight of the world seemed to be pressing down all around her and the funny thing was, she'd been in school for less than thirty days. *I wish I could talk to someone,* Sunshine bemoaned, as she walked around campus in the imaginary bubble that she created for herself by pushing everyone away. Without her self-described six feet rule or imaginary bubble, Sunshine was not sure if she would have the tenacity to ever leave her dorm room.

During the days since school started, Sunshine had quickly developed a labyrinth of socially inept tools. Whenever in the presence of her classmates who would try to engage her in light conversation, Sunshine would react with sweaty palms as she frantically tried to control her breathing. Thoughts would rush into her mind, giving energy to the notion that if anyone tried to shake her hand they would discover her over-moist hands and the fact that she was a walking, skin-encased bacterial petri dish.

Soon Sunshine found herself walking around campus with gloves on to keep from shaking hands and receiving any microbial germs from the unnecessary hand shaking ritual that young people engage in. The gloves only exacerbated her sweaty hands and therefore created the need for the gloves in the first place to hide her sweaty palms. Whatever the reason, Sunshine couldn't figure out why her fellow classmates went from having that starstruck glow in their eyes to staring at her with the side-eye reserved for people who wear winter coats in the middle of an August heatwave.

I realize that I may have some undiagnosed anxiety problems, Sunshine thought to herself, but somehow she just blew off the notion by lathering up her mind with the soothing words of comfort that **everybody got a little crazy in them**. In such a short span of time, the only thing that was certain in her young life besides the ridiculous amount of school assignments became the familiar face of her little bird friend. Sunshine could hardly hold in her joy each morning as she etched out minutes before class to visit and talk with Mr. Bird.

"Hello, Mr. Bird!" Sunshine would squeal in what she imagined her bird voice as she found her faithful friend always sitting on his perch seemingly awaiting her greeting. For the most part, Sunshine played a game of silent observation as she watched Mr. Bird scurry around his nest. Then one day, she noticed that he did not fly away when she approached the window. This attracted Sunshine to the little creature even more and made her feel like she had finally found another loyal friend on campus besides Belle. Sunshine had always been attracted to animals and their ability to capture the heart without the use of words. With Mr. Bird, Sunshine felt some type of bond and found herself commanded to their secret window rendezvous having no idea why this little bird was so fascinating to her young eyes.

One fall day before the leaves fell from the trees on campus, the bird, who had taken several weeks to expeditiously prepare his nest for his family, looked at Sunshine from outside the windowsill and pleaded with his tiny beady eyes, **"Can I stay here?"**

It was the first time Sunshine had imagined what she thought was Mr. Bird talking directly to her. Just to make sure, Sunshine twirled around abruptly to be certain no one else was in the room. "I know this bird didn't just ask me if he can crash in my room?" Sunshine inquired to no one in particular. Luckily, the out-of-this-world request was delivered in a one-on-one situation instead of in the middle of campus, which would have attracted an undetermined amount of attention. The reading and homework assignments and copious amounts of research papers were nerve-wracking all by themselves, and somehow Sunshine found it hard to believe that she had sunk to that dark place where people resort to talking to birds.

"I hope you know normal people don't sweat like you?" the bird responded.

Immediately Sunshine could feel her sweat glands activate, and sweat started running down her upper lip and rapidly toward her hands and onto her fingertips. In her young mind it seemed like her new bird friend chirped out the declaration, "You're never going to be anything."

"Why can't you be awesome like your brother?" she imagined the bird casually chirping.

I know for a fact that I'm alone in the room, Sunshine mused. In fact, no one had entered the room unannounced since she had sprinted from her last class of the day and the protective company of her roommate in the cafeteria for their evening meal together. But somehow the voice she was hearing was as present and real as two people facing each other engaged in a conversation. Since Sunshine was certain that no one had entered the room, she suddenly placed all her attention on the bird sitting on the windowsill quietly going about his business without regard to her full blown meltdown.

"Why are you looking at me like that?" the bird nonchalantly inquired. "All I'm trying to do here is build my nest and create a resting place for my family."

As Sunshine looked at his beak, she quickly surmised that every time his little bird mouth moved she felt that a message was being transferred to her mind. *Can this little sparrow be talking to me or am I losing my mind?* Sunshine thought to herself. The confrontation with Mr. Bird left her standing motionless in the midst of an epic internal implosion, when she heard the sound of a key in the door.

Belle was over the moon about being selected to join the world famous school choir, and eager to share her excitement with everyone in her path. With the news perched precariously, ready to drip excitedly off her lips at the mere sight of her roomie, it suddenly struck Belle as strange that she felt the presence of her roommate in the room even though she was nowhere to be found.

"Sunshine would never leave the light on or the window open if she left the room!" Belle moaned as she headed to close the only window in the room. As she approached the window, out of the corner of her eye Belle glimpsed a bird sitting in his nest that flew away before she even waved her hand to shoo him. Turning around from the window and completely unbothered by a bird sitting on her dorm ledge, Belle became determined to check every single hiding area of any normal claustrophobic college living space for her roommate. After checking the tiny closet that would seem too tight for the storage of a human body, Belle heard some weeping noises coming from under Sunshine's bed. The thought seemed bizarre to check under the bed, but with no other place to look, Belle decided to take a peek.

"Roommate, what on earth are you doing hiding under the bed?" Belle screamed.

I have no answer, Sunshine thought to herself.

The question itself seemed more irrational than any answer one could pluck out of the sky with some imagined superpower. *With all the homework being shoved down my throat, it would seem counterintuitive to spend precious time playing hide and seek from my roommate*, Sunshine pondered.

Sunshine had a slight inclination to respond to the looming question and share with her roommate the conversations she was having in her mind with a bird on their windowsill, but no words came spewing from her lips. Sunshine's brain had shut off the response mechanism attached to her vocal chords and nothing audible was able to come out of her mouth.

In no uncertain terms she wanted to yell, *No, you found me hiding under my bed because it actually felt like the earth was coming apart at the seams and our dormitory room was the epicenter of the earthquake. Somehow, the ebb and flow of the neurons, protons, cells and other minutiae that make up the human body scattered in every direction possible at the sound of the alarm in my mind.*

Run!

Hide.

The size of the imagined earthquake going on in my head had suddenly reached an epic 9.0 on the Richter scale and every cell in my body received the memo to evacuate except for my outer body or what I consider to be the physical me. Literally, I was left standing in the middle of my dorm room as collateral damage as every inch of my insides decided to run for cover due to the words coming from the beak of a lone bird on our windowsill.

Imagining that she was sharing her darkest secret with her roommate, Sunshine resumed with her thoughts. *With the delayed reaction of a runner unable to hear the starter gun at a track meet, I stumbled forward and found myself taking cover under my bed, unapologetically dazed by the voices forcing their way into my head.* Yet, when Sunshine opened her mouth to deliver this outrageous message of fight or flight and how she eventually ended up under her bed, no words found their way past her vocal cords except for her pained moans.

The experience and perhaps the nightmare of communicating with a seemingly random bird shook Sunshine to her core. As she sheepishly looked into the eyes of Belle for support, Sunshine simultaneously welcomed the awkward comfort of the confined space under the bed as a place of safety from the voices that were trying to inhabit her mind.

"Sunshine, you're making me really scared. Please come from under the bed and talk to me," Belle pleaded. Eventually, Belle coaxed Sunshine to squeeze her frame from under the bed. Initially, Belle was prepared to fuss and scold her roommate and remind her that they were no longer high school kids but college women. The words were sitting on her lips waiting for discharge when she happened to glimpse the frightened look on Sunshine's face. Instead, the two ladies just sat on the bed and hugged each other in complete silence as they realized that college life for one of them was rapidly about to take a drastic detour.

The task of being a college student over the next several weeks was not easy, but with sheer determination and lots of luck, Sunshine was somehow able to tap dance around her classes with enough acuity to have passing grades in all subjects by the end of midterms. Even with her looming success in the classroom, Sunshine soon realized that it was actually getting harder and harder each day to accomplish simple tasks like teeth brushing. It wasn't that she didn't want to brush her teeth; after all, Sunshine had endured two years of braces for her beautiful smile. Yet, she didn't feel the beauty that perfectly straight teeth were promised to bring her malcontented heart. The rationale jumping around in her head was, *If you don't brush your teeth, it will increase the probability of not having to talk to anybody.*

The various internal discussions were insanely real and lasted for hours, sometimes over a very singular and simple topic such as whether or not to brush her teeth or how many times she should wash her hands per hour. The conversations had increased from the seemingly innocent question by Mr. Bird at the start of the school year to full-blown war in her mind on a daily basis. The constant talking and incessant voices were starting to affect her grades as Sunshine grew easily tired from all the commotion in her head and invisible dialogue.

Sunshine would shake her head furiously like a baby trying to dislocate a few coins from a piggy bank to no avail, hoping to reduce the noise going on in her insides. Unfortunately, shaking her head only seemed to increase the pounding in her head, almost as payback for trying to interfere with the noise. Turning up the television or radio volume to quiet whatever chatter was going on in her head only became a quick fix. Sunshine soon found out that the voices simply increased their volume as if they were determined to be heard at any costs.

"Who does she think she is, turning up the radio?"

"I can hardly hear myself talk above the television noise!"

"Well, how on earth would this poor child know whether to brush her teeth or not if we don't talk about it and come to a consensus?"

The mind babble and jibber jab were constant and could center on one innate or insignificant situation for hours on end or until somehow, mercifully, Sunshine would catch a break and fall asleep.

Or so she thought.

Sunshine quickly found out that the act of going to bed or trying to fall asleep did not necessarily determine that she would get any rest. There were times when the voices became the loudest right in the middle of her sleep...

"Wake up!"

"Wake up!"

"We're not finished discussing why your hands are so sweaty."

"Who told you to turn off the lights?"

"No one loves you."

On and on the booming noises would detonate in her head without warning and last for as long as they cared to. It seemed to Sunshine that she was slowly being evicted out of her own mind and relocated to the basement of her body. Without a doubt, she knew the consequences of taking up residence in the lower extremities of her body without her mind was surely a recipe for disaster and an invitation for inevitable death. Yet, she had no clue how to rescue her mind from its temporary shelter and reposition it back to its birth home.

Sunshine longed to be back home in her right mind, living a life full of joy. Over and over, she pondered, *What is the secret to finding joy in the midst of this crazy storm that I am experiencing?* She often wondered how on earth she gave up so much real estate in her head to a flock of birds that seemed so harmless. The funny thing was, she knew that she wanted to get home to "herself," but she no longer had any earthly clue which way home was.

By the week before final exams, it took practically everything in Sunshine's body to convince herself to get out of bed. Yes, she knew she was in the engineering program and aimlessly lying in bed could not be tolerated. But getting her mind to cooperate with her body was becoming as daunting as building Trump's wall across the Mexican border.

Sunshine wanted to scream at the top of her lungs, "What is wrong with you?" But she instinctively knew the question would be split between the new occupants of her mind and herself. If she tried to speak up, the incessant banging in her head would start to roar. Incredibly, with all the chaos going on, she was able to keep everything in her life patched together and somehow hide the birds in her head from everyone on campus until the week of final exams.

"Sunshine, why do you hide us way up here in your head?" the birds one day implored.

"We want to meet your friends," they suddenly declared. One way or another, Sunshine knew from their recent outburst that she was finally at war with the birds that had taken up space in her head. However, she had come to battle this newly-declared attack on her life with knives while the enemy was stockpiled with missiles pointed at her forehead. Sunshine was extremely embarrassed that she had to keep such an awful secret to herself…the simple truth was that she needed help. She was finally tired of all of the noise going on in her mind and did not believe she could make it home to the safety of her dorm room or her windowsill another day. But before she could talk to a mental health professional, right there in the university cafeteria, her well-kept secret and nest of loud talking birds collided right smack in front of the cafeteria lady, Mrs. Owens.

Sunshine only briefly heard Mrs. Owens announce that eggs were temporarily off the menu for breakfast as she grabbed her tray and utensils. On the surface, it didn't seem like the end of the world. The solution was actually quite logical. *Just ask for more grits or extra wheat toast and ignore the fact that the cafeteria is out of eggs,* Sunshine briefly declared to herself. Then, Sunshine remembered her twisted plot to eat eggs every day with the rationale being, *If I eat the eggs, perhaps the birds will take it personally and eventually relocate to a less hostile environment.*

The simple lack of eggs for breakfast sent Sunshine into a fit of uncontrollable crying that landed her on the floor of the cafeteria with her jacket over her head to disappear from the gathering crowd.

"Who on earth is that under their jacket?" cried the growing crowd of onlookers.

Suddenly, the noises inside Sunshine's young mind stopped all the inward chatter and made room for the silence. After a brief moment, the bird from the windowsill cleared his throat and declared, "My name is Mr. Bird," albeit to his audience of one.

"See, I told you all I wanted to do was meet your friends," whispered Mr. Bird. "Now look what you made me do," he scoffed.

Mr. Bird remained without emotion as Sunshine laid in a motionless heap on the floor. "The whole school is going to know about me soon enough," he calmly stated. That was the last thing Sunshine heard as she drifted away into a complete meltdown of anguish and cries for help.

When she finally awoke, Sunshine quickly realized she was not in the familiar space of her dorm room. Due to the machines surrounding her bedside and the sight of her roommate Belle sniffling quietly in the corner, she surmised she had been rushed to the hospital.

Trying to process the last twenty-four hours was a challenge, as it was all still pretty fuzzy. *At least the voices are not bothering me,* Sunshine thought to herself. Over the constant buzz of the machines in the room, Sunshine somehow found the strength to roll over in her bed and dispatch her roommate to purchase an egg sandwich from the hospital café, just in case the machines and tubes sticking out of her body needed some help with her recovery.

Without fanfare the door was slowly pushed open and the chaplain of the university, Pastor Belfore Mullins, walked into the room with a smile brighter than a 100-watt light bulb. Skipping all the small talk, he cleared his throat and went straight into his announcement.

"Sunshine, I've come to your bedside to tell you that the breakdown you suffered is for your good, God's glory and someone else's benefit."

Sunshine was purely dumbfounded by the toxic air quality in the room since the chaplain's arrival and released a coughing spell as a futile defense. After looking up and seeing that the good reverend was not jilted by her coughing microbes, Sunshine found her voice and asked her first question since arriving at the hospital.

"Pastor Mullins, how is my getting sick at the start of my young adult life for my good?" Sunshine pleaded. She cautiously continued, "College is supposed to be the best four years of my life. I'm barely ten steps into my freshman year and here comes the hurricane of my life."

Instead of answering the question that his bold statement had elicited, the chaplain deflected to regain control of the situation with his urgent message. "Sunshine, we had no choice but to call your grandmother. Your situation is not something you can make disappear with a couple of aspirins," he insisted.

In an awkward attempt to calm the fears regarding the magnitude of what Sunshine was facing, Pastor Mullins guardedly continued. "You have an illness that cannot be fixed in the middle of final exams or in the confines of your dorm room. When you are well and back to yourself, you are more than welcome to return to the university and finish up your studies."

Sunshine clearly heard the open invitation to return to school from the chaplain but that was not what had the tears flowing down her face like an open faucet. Everyone in the room saw the tears and, interpreting their meaning, rushed to hug and comfort her and to stifle the real question in the room. However, Sunshine was actually stuck on the words from the chaplain, "back to yourself."

Those words reverberated in her ears as if her illness was a conscious decision to take a leave of absence from her own body. Sunshine wanted to scream at the peeling paint chips on the wall because she felt like no one else could hear her voice or feel her excruciating pain. In sheer exasperation, Sunshine turned to the wall and shouted, "When I look deep into myself, there's no me looking back at me – all I see is a bunch of thoughts and unexplained weird behaviors. It's as if I'm all stuck inside myself with no way out."

Looking directly at the chaplain, Sunshine yelled, "So, how am I so lucky to eventually escape this black hole of a journey and one day come back to myself? On some level, it would seem that everyone would be scurrying to go back and forth through this portal of 'selves' to escape life's complexities from time to time." With no answer floating around in the room, Sunshine eventually grew tired of her eye matrix with the chaplain and the awkward looks she received from the nurse and her roommate due to her sudden outburst. In fact, she simply longed for the medication the nurse had recently given her to take effect so she could drift quietly off to sleep.

The sleeping pill was taking its sweet time to work its magic and transport Sunshine to a place of solace from all the screaming that had resumed in her head. So the voice of doubt decided to chirp in with a few last minute words of despair and discouragement.

"You'll never be free of this…"

"You'll never be free of this…"

"You'll never get back to yourself."

Sunshine hurriedly back-pedaled out of the depths of her tormented cocoon as she struggled to focus on the words that had come out of the chaplain's mouth. Although she was drifting off to sleep, she summoned all her energy to concentrate on the words "back to myself" that she imagined the chaplain was repeating over and over. She forced her eyes open long enough to try and find solace from the words she thought were dripping off of his lips. But instead of hearing the sweet phrase, "back to myself," and the hope for a full recovery that it inspired, the voices continued their incessant pounding and shouting in an unruly fashion.

"You'll never be free of this."

"You'll never be free of this."

Somehow, in the midst of all the psychobabble, Sunshine started to repeat the words over and over that her grandmother would whisper throughout the house whenever life became too much for her to bear its burden. Her words came slicing through the noise as she fell into the first peaceful sleep in days.

"Prayer changes things!"

"Prayer changes things!"

CHAPTER 3
Misdiagnosis

Getting the call from the chaplain of the university was the last thing on Queen Elizabeth's mind as she was preparing her disrespectful macaroni and cheese dish to take to the monthly church mothers' potluck. As she sprinkled her secret ingredient into the pan just before placing the casserole into the oven, Queen let out a childish giggle as she thought about the fact that it had been twenty years since she'd cooked anything besides the "dish" for her church family. Although Queen had been cooking full meals for her family since the tender age of eight years old, all memories of her delicious melt-in-your-mouth collard greens and shake-your-head-at-your-momma fried chicken went out the window when people tasted her macaroni and cheese. The infamous dilemma between the church mothers and their cooking skills was finally sealed regarding at least one particular item on the menu by the now retired Pastor Lawrence during the worship service some two decades earlier. The pastor, in some cosmic moment, sensed the conflict and competition between the church mothers and suddenly declared from the pulpit, "Don't nobody else bring any more macaroni and cheese up in this church as long as Church Mother Queen is alive."

The joke was still fresh in Queen's mind as she hurried to wipe her hands and grab the ringing phone before it went to voicemail. Queen knew if she didn't grab the phone before the fourth ring, it would jump into voicemail and she would have to wait until her grandson took time out of his young life to visit and retrieve her messages. In Queen's mind, *All this technology stuff was for young folk and know-it-all millennial babies.*

"Hello, this is Church Mother Queen. I'm blessed and highly favored." Queen held tight to her distinctive greeting and answered the phone in this manner on purpose. She knew that her church family had become familiar with the greeting and were totally unbothered. On the other hand, the greeting had become her personal wall to filter out the callers who had ill intentions to secretly get at her social security check or banking information.

Slowly, Chaplain Mullins cleared his throat and cautiously proceeded with the news that never got any easier even though he was approaching fifteen years in his capacity as the chaplain of the university. *Lord, how do I tell yet another family that their child is sick?* he thought. *The task of making the difficult phone call to a family member or guardian and breaking the news that the young vibrant student entrusted to our care to educate and transform into an adult is now in trouble or deceased was the hardest part of the job,* he silently sighed.

Not knowing what to say in response to such an over-the-top phone greeting, the chaplain lost all the finesse that his doctoral degree afforded him and awkwardly blurted out the name listed as Sunshine's guardian. "Mother Queen, your grandbaby Sunshine is hearing voices and she was rushed to Huntsville Hospital for observation."

The urgency in the chaplain's voice was very familiar to Queen, as she had received countless calls from church members and friends who had gotten in trouble over the years and needed her help. Although the conversation with the chaplain didn't have much dialogue to it, his words reverberated to Queen's ear as she stumbled to her favorite chair. The memories of holding Sunshine in her arms and rocking her to sleep as a premature baby who was determined to be born despite the fact that she was seven weeks early oozed into Queen's mind.

As Queen continued to listen to the chaplain, she mostly responded with her typical signature statement which always included, "Really," and "Is that so?" Oblivious to the fact that Queen had already made up her mind that she would be leaving that night to get to her precious baby, the chaplain went on and on about how Sunshine had a meltdown in the cafeteria and the other peculiar events that led to her hospitalization. Queen listened distractedly as her thoughts were far away from the words coming out of the chaplain's mouth. She thought about how quickly the years had passed since her last visit to the hallowed grounds where her very first grandchild, Lil Son, had received his college degree.

"Lord, has it really been ten years since I've been to Alabama?" Queen whispered the words in a restrained murmur under her breath as she hurried the chaplain off the phone to pack her few garments and her precious Bible.

Without much preparation for the crisis that showed up with little advance notice, Queen knew that her fastest option to get to her grandchild would be to hop on an airplane. But the memory of her last plane ride and how violently it shook as she crossed the ocean from burying her Panamanian husband in his native land kept Queen from making the friendly skies an option. With great haste and dispatch, Queen decided that she would tackle her dilemma regarding transportation with a concept called the Megabus. The decision to ride the bus was final, and Queen rushed to finish preparations to leave later that evening.

Her departure would not be a moment sooner than she cleaned her spotless house from top to bottom. Queen was old school and even if she didn't want to, she knew her upbringing would have her cleaning and mopping before leaving town. On some kind of level, the wisdom of her elders had taught her the simple truth that you cannot run off to fix someone else's mess if your own house is not in order.

It was truly a miracle that Queen didn't miss her bus later that evening as she heeded the lightbulb idea in her head to stop by the corner store for a honeybun and some Jolly Ranchers. Queen knew her doctor would not approve but it was all she had to comfort her nerves as she embarked on this emergency trip.

After taking her time to navigate the high steps to board the bus, she stealthily walked down the aisle looking for the perfect seat. Upon final inspection of the whole bus and feeling assured that it harbored no known terrorist, she finally raced her way back to the front and settled on the second-row seat directly across from the bus driver. Once Queen glimpsed his squinty little eyes upon boarding, she knew it would be her personal mission to keep an eye or two on his driving skills.

She quietly squeezed into her seat and pulled out her favorite pillow, deciding it was time to find a passage from her precious Bible to calm her overactive brain thoughts. After such a hectic day, she longed for a scripture to warm her heart and slowly put her to sleep for the remainder of the trip. Suddenly, instead of drifting off to sleep, the nightmare scenario of riding a bus across the country unfolded as a young voluptuous woman with a newborn baby decided to choose the unoccupied seat next to Queen.

The real problem did not start until the bus pulled away from the New York Port Authority bus station and the young lady started telling her unedited life story in full detail. The almost unbearable eighteen-hour trip from the gritty streets of New York to the rolling hills of Huntsville, Alabama was intermittently sprinkled with the endless stories told by her temporary seatmate, Passion. Queen was completely baffled that anyone could be so inclined to unleash so much verbal punishment on the ears of someone with a single-minded mission and no room to care. Queen was beyond aghast that her unexpected seat companion was only twenty years old and could possibly have a life story that would still have dips and turns as the bus pulled up to the university.

Leaving Passion's latest story in mid-sentence, Queen hurriedly grabbed her suitcase and the box that contained her precious church hat and adjusted her body to press past her companion of almost twenty-four hours. Queen imagined that Passion had already told her everything that had ever happened in her young life even though her mouth seemed to still be moving as she made her way off the bus. Although Queen was known as a "fixer of all things" in her neighborhood, she found it almost impossible to offer Passion any guidance because of the information overload she had received. The two ladies quietly parted ways as Queen stepped off the bus at the campus stop. Somehow, Queen felt that there could be more plots and twists to Passion's story even though they said goodbye and waved to each other as the bus pulled off.

Nonetheless, Queen couldn't use another minute to think about a random seatmate and her crying baby. Queen knew she had a date with destiny to get to the bedside of her grandbaby and let her know that everything would be alright. But, as she waited for her Uber driver on a nearby bench that faced the campus church, a flood of memories rushed back from the far corners of her mind. For the first time since receiving the phone call from the school administrator, Queen chuckled. She quietly reflected on how quickly ten years had flown by since her first born grandchild had graduated from this prestigious university.

"It wasn't easy," Queen whispered, as she remembered that she'd had way more prayers than money to help educate her grandbaby. Queen closed her eyes briefly as she thought about her relentless search to find the largest hat possible to wear to the graduation to showcase the prayers and tears that made the journey worthwhile. "But, the good Lord made a way somehow," fell from Queen's lips as she opened her eyes and noticed that several birds had gathered around her park bench.

"I ain't got no food and you can't stay here," Queen yelled, as she flapped her hands and shooed the birds from her presence.

Now, where is my Uber? Queen thought, cringing at the idea of what her life would be like without the use of the rideshare platform.

As she followed the detailed instructions of Chaplain Mullins, she quickly exited her Uber and made her way to the third floor of the hospital, which was reserved for patients involved in psychotic breakdowns. Although Queen had buried two husbands, nothing seemed to prepare her to see her precious grandbaby in a situation where she would be out of her mind. Queen racked her own mind back and forth as she excruciatingly tried to figure out who could be the black sheep in her family with the "crazy gene." After going up and down the bloodline for three generations, Queen was exhausted but satisfied that only regular crazy people had infiltrated her family tree, folks that just couldn't possibly get right even with a little monthly government handout. "Even free money is not enough for them to find a way to sit down and be quiet," Queen chuckled.

Coincidentally, the minute Queen took a gander over at the family tree of her daughter's choice in a spouse, she knew she had hit pay dirt. Queen snickered as she recalled the special family members on the other side of the tree that needed to sit down in a jail cell for a few months to catch their breath. She whispered somewhat boldly to herself, "Crazy runs up and down my son-in-law's tree line," just as the elevator door opened onto the behavioral health unit.

Queen stepped off the elevator onto the third floor of the hospital for the first time and was completely taken aback by the outpouring of love and the sheer volume of students just hanging out in the lobby. It was a solid two days after "the episode," as the fallout in the cafeteria became known, and yet it was still the hottest topic around campus. To Church Mother Queen, who had spent the majority of her eighty-five years on earth fighting life's struggles alone, the display of love toward her precious granddaughter was irresistible. The impact of the moment caused Queen to stop in her tracks just five steps off of the elevator. Not knowing which way to turn to get to her baby, Queen just stood still.

Out of the corner of her eye, Belle saw the striking resemblance to her roomie in the elderly woman frozen at the elevator door and ran over to introduce herself.

"Hi, I'm Belle. I'm Sunshine's roommate. It is a pleasure to finally meet you."

Because of all the hilarious late-night stories that Belle had endured over the last couple of months regarding her roommate's grandmother, she somehow felt a special bond to Queen as she unceremoniously grabbed her by the arm and held on tight. "It's a pleasure to meet you," is all Queen could utter as she wondered where on earth her grandbaby was being held hostage.

As if reading her mind, Belle clutched her new friend and unofficial godmother around her waist and brought her directly to her roommate's door. Finally seeing her baby since hearing the news of the breakdown made Queen run to her bedside and collapse into her arms. Neither woman talked as they continued their embrace for several minutes. The only thing that they shared were the commingling of their tears and simultaneously beating hearts.

Queen finally pulled back, leaned into Sunshine's ear and whispered, "Baby, even in this silence that we are sharing, I have a story to tell you." Queen gently exhaled as she described to her youngest grandbaby her long standing promise… "All I want in this world is to keep you. Keep you from hurting too much, keep you from any pain and somehow keep you from the pitfalls of life." Queen leaned back toward her granddaughter and gently wiped the tears from her eyes. She hugged her without applying much pressure, as if she was handling a newborn baby. Somehow, Queen felt that if she squeezed her precious granddaughter too tight, she would be blamed if Sunshine lost any more of her normal thoughts.

After what seemed like an eternity, Queen turned back to the doctors for answers and Sunshine scurried back to her inner thoughts.

CHAPTER 4
Take Your Meds, Please

Those who are well have no need of a physician,
but those who are sick...
Matthew 9:12

Dear Diary...

How on earth did I get here?

Where am I?

I'm shouting at the top of my lungs, waiting in vain for someone, practically anyone to come rescue me. My questions are directed out into the big wide universe, and somehow it is preloaded with several possible answers. Turning my head to survey my surroundings, nothing seems even remotely familiar. The walls are lime green, a color perhaps chosen to help one forget time as it constantly marches forward. The walls are bare except for the unhurried, timeless peeling of the awful green paint.

I wanted to run.

Get back to my life. The life that I once knew. Somehow, life as I know it in the moment is squarely in this lime green room and the bed I am lying in. Why can't I move my body? "Well, for one thing," the voices respond, "you're restrained to your bed because you cannot control yourself."

Instantly, I try to rise up out of the bed to prove the voices in my head wrong. But I'm strapped to the bed like a prisoner of war. I have no answers and I'm too tired to keep asking questions. I feel like the only constant in the world is the steadfast beating of the machine that's monitoring my heart rate and blood pressure.

As Sunshine slowly regained consciousness, she came to the realization that her surroundings were not the precious cocoon of her dormitory room. The only thing that remained constant in her hospital life was the loving presence of her grandmother, who had remained by her side from almost the very moment of her ordeal. Instead of thankfulness that she was still among the land of the living, nothing but guilt rushed through her body as she laid on her bed and helplessly observed time march on at its synchronized beat. With slight trepidation she found the courage to peer out from all the wires sticking out of her body.

Suddenly remembering her massive derailment episode, Sunshine fixated her gaze on the only window in the room. With tears gathering at the corners of her eyes, she dreamed of what could have been done to prevent the Showtime at the Apollo moment that was revealed in front of her schoolmates in the cafeteria.

Could I have told someone that I was hearing voices?

Why did I allow those pesky voices into my head?
It must be my fault that I am sick.
What will the kids at school think about me?

All these bothersome little thoughts came rushing into Sunshine's brain flow right at a time when she should have been in a zone of complete rest, thinking about absolutely nothing but healing. Yet, as Sunshine looked around the hospital room, all she saw were people staring back at her with gleaming eyes and the heartfelt desire for her to be well.

How can I ever stop the constant barrage of questions from my family that keep stabbing my mind and plunging me into darkness? Sunshine thought. As her own questions continued to flood her mind, Sunshine suddenly felt the warmth and caressing of her hand by her grandmother.

Queen softly whispered, "I need you to be well, Sunshine." After a long pause Sunshine looked up with the saddest of eyes and responded, "I'm doing my best, Grandma, but I can't stay sane just for you, okay?"

Without waiting on her grandmother's reaction, Sunshine disappeared into herself because somehow, she knew deep down inside that her crazy was no longer just an irritating quirk...like it was to anyone who got close for a short spell.

Ironically, the doctors continued to reassure Sunshine on an almost daily basis that she would be going home "just as soon as you return to yourself." Sunshine, on the other hand, couldn't help but notice that her college friends thought she held the magic wand and the answer to her very own dilemma of when she would return to herself.

Sunshine slowly exhaled as she looked around the room and took in the magnitude of her new normal and long road ahead to recovery. She continued her internal dialogue: *Most of my visitors stop by my hospital room and expect me to pick up my bed and walk out the psychiatric ward because they spoke a few words of encouragement over my life. Well, it doesn't work like that, Sherlock!* She secretly chuckled to herself.

If it was that easy to get back to myself, would I really choose to stay in this place of discomfort and confusion? Sunshine was in complete pity-party mode at this point and felt no reason to stop talking inside her head even as her bedside was surrounded with friends and well-wishers. So, without anyone's approval she continued her inward whining. *I had perfect attendance, made the Dean's List, kept my room tidy and even enjoyed going to church. I was not always stuck inside of myself. Or inside my selves,* she corrected.

"I wasn't only crazy," she unapologetically stated out loud in a commanding voice that quieted all the other conversations in the room.

"Oh no, Baby, no one thinks that you're..." Queen struggled to find the right word.

"Say it, Grandma," Sunshine pleaded. "Say the big fat word that's screaming out loud and no one is giving it any attention or a voice in the room."

She exhaled.

Queen abruptly removed her hand from Sunshine's and remained silent.

"Never mind," Sunshine scoffed, "I will say the word. I will give a voice to my pain."

"I'm crazy!" Sunshine yelled with all the strength she could muster.

The words shot out like a cannon and bounced from wall to wall in search of a resting place. Sunshine swiftly dragged her eyes around the room, searching the blank faces staring back at her. She shifted her gaze back out the window as if to give the one word that was sworn to secrecy while she was asleep permission to land. The room was in complete silence as grandmother Queen and Belle stood absolutely motionless, unable to catch up to the fact that the big "C" word had been finally uttered out loud.

In that singular moment of uncertainty in the room, Sunshine realized that there was no way she would ever be able to squeeze the enormousness of herself back into her tiny broken body. For all she knew, her secret was out all over campus and being spread behind her back like wildfire. Even in her fragile state of mind, it made sense to verbalize the same word that was most likely being batted around campus and throughout the tiny enclave of Madison county with reckless abandon. The only difference in the equation was the fact that the silent "C" word was simply not being uttered in her presence. Period!

Turning in the direction of her grandmother and the ugly green wall behind her, Sunshine mumbled ever so softly, "It's ok, Grandma, nobody gets anybody else…it's almost impossible. On some level we're all stuck inside ourselves and our own birdcage of thoughts and imagination."

Not knowing what else could possibly spew from Sunshine's mouth, Queen hurriedly sat on the edge of the bed to keep from falling as she tried to take it all in, including the forbidden "C" word. It was hard for Queen to process the mental picture of her perfect little family being shattered by reality and that powerful thing called genetics that was flowing through the family tree.

As Sunshine looked into Queen's eyes, she felt the pain and hardship that her illness was causing her grandmother. She decided to speak again, although this time she spoke with a heart full of compassion. "Grandma, I apologize that it will be no fun hanging out with me anymore since I will only be stuck in my head. But, imagine if you were actually stuck inside your own head with no way out, with no chance of escape or moment of sanity, because that is exactly what my new life is going to be like."

For the first time since arriving at the bedside of her precious grandbaby, Queen experienced an intense desire to cry. But as much as she pushed, no tears developed in her eyes. It seemed like Queen had floated into town on pure adrenaline and prayers once she'd received the phone call regarding her baby's sudden illness. Miraculously, even after being by Sunshine's bedside for almost two weeks now, the tears still had not shown up. "Lord, why can't I cry?" Queen whispered.

Then, without any fanfare or noisy introduction, just as the illicit question dripped off of her lips in prayer, a tear started to puddle and gather at the rim of her eyelids. Not tears of despair or regret, because Queen knew on a deeper level through her years of wisdom that she had to show up to the hospital as a warrior ready for battle to fight for her baby. But somehow, today the tears finally started to flow freely and without permission as she awoke to the realization that her precious little baby had grown up before her eyes.

After a brief moment, Queen slowly wiped her eyes and smiled profusely in a fragile attempt to send all her positive energy toward her baby. She grasped the magnitude of what a full, uncontrollable meltdown could cause in the hospital room and decided against it.

"It's okay to cry, Grandma," Sunshine softly whispered.

"Not now, baby. My tears have no expiration date. If you are blessed to live long enough, you will find that the tears will come whenever they feel like it." Queen had a secret lying on her own bosom, but she knew she wouldn't be able to turn off the waterworks if she started to think about how little time she had left with her grandbaby and precious circle of church friends.

"Not now, baby. I've got to be strong for you," Queen cooed as she leaned over and held her precious Sunshine close to her heart. And just like that, Queen changed the subject and avoided her very own tsunami by the accidental revealing of her secret.

"How are you feeling today, my sweet butter biscuit?" Queen inquired as she tried desperately to lighten the mood in the room. Sunshine knew that whenever her grandmother called her by food names...my lemon drop, my loaf of bread, she was definitely trying to change the subject.

Sunshine wanted with all her might to hug her grandma tight and erase any pain that her illness was causing. She wanted to tell her that she was getting much better, because that was supposed to be the end story of illness. On some level, illness was usually a traumatic story told in the past tense by a thankful and relieved survivor.

> Friend: *Dude, I haven't seen you in ages. Where have you been?*
>
> Me: *Let me tell you what happened to me recently. I was sick as a dog. I thought I was going to die. It took three days for the fever to break.*
> *but, by the grace of God, I made it.*

Somehow, telling any near-death experience can elicit nervous laughter. But instead of trying to make jokes with those gathered around her hospital bed, Sunshine was frantically trying to think of what a normal person's response would be to such a simple question...**how are you today?**

Hurry and answer the question, Sunshine scolded herself.

"Must you turn every single question into a thesis opportunity?" the voices brazenly added.

Immediately and without any fanfare she awkwardly blurted out, **"Patched up!"** This sudden reply was Sunshine's feeble attempt to finally answer the excruciating question, "How are you feeling today?" Somehow, she didn't see the point in saying, "I'm fine." *If everyone is actually waiting with bated breath for me to one day come back to myself, well, today is not that day,* she mused.

Unexpectedly, everyone in the room repeated the words "patched up" and proceeded to laugh uncontrollably. It appeared that what she'd said was funny, so she laughed because everyone else had. She locked eyes with Belle from across the room as she desperately waited for someone to run to her side and rescue her. No one came.

Seeing the helplessness in Belle's pupils, Sunshine held her gaze on Belle's face just long enough to watch her eyes return to the awkward admiration of the lime green paint on the walls. *Maybe, just maybe, if I could just bring my lips to say and do whatever normal people say and do, then perhaps I could even become one*, Sunshine thought.

It's not like people are beating down my door for my autograph or anything, Sunshine acknowledged. *Maybe, if I was carjacked or shot multiple times in a case of mistaken identity and died on the way to the hospital, it might warrant an Instagram post or something. Then I could possibly be declared a martyr. Martyrs make great heroes and mean something to most people.*

This constant attack of dialogue within herself was Sunshine's daily routine of random thoughts running through her mind. The only thing that frequently interrupted her monotonous thoughts was the synchronized clockwork of the nurses coming in and out of the room to stick her, poke her, check her blood pressure or draw her blood.

With everyone in the room securely in their own thoughts, the door noisily swung open and interrupted all the silent conversations. In walked Dr. Chung, the attending physician and the one person that Sunshine was gradually opening up to more and more each day. Dr. Chung had previously shared with her that he had arrived in America at fourteen years of age without speaking much English. However, with arduous work and determination, he graduated from medical school by the time he was twenty-eight years old. It was the sharing of his back story that made Dr. Chung the chosen one in Sunshine's eyes and caused her to light up whenever he walked in the room.

"I have some good news for you and some great news," Dr. Chung smiled as he approached her bedside. "What is the news, Dr. Chung?" Sunshine eagerly inquired. After being locked up in the hospital for almost a month, she sat up quickly in bed at the thought of good news. With bated breath, she crossed the fingers of her right hand under her blanket, hoping the news would consist of an exit plan.

"Well, sometimes medicine is developed for one thing and ends up being just as good for another ailment in our body," Dr. Chung explained. "There is a new drug on the market that will seek to quiet the voices and not make you so lethargic and sleepy most of the day. What do you think, Sunshine?" he inquired. "You think you want to give these pills a try?" Even though he was talking to Sunshine, for some reason he was looking directly at her grandmother for the response.

Sunshine quickly dismissed the eyeball matrix between the two and emphatically interjected, "I ain't taking no more pills once I leave this hospital. I'm feeling absolutely fine. I'm almost back to my old self. The pills have done their job. And I thank you and this fine bird cage of a hospital very much."

Sunshine continued her rant. "I have been poked, probed and examined every which way like an alien from outer space. It's time I get back to myself and pick up the life I left on the cafeteria floor."

Although Queen realized that her baby was all grown up, she shot the doctor a quick glance and a head nod to reassure him to ignore the words coming out of her granddaughter's mouth. Queen decided almost instantly and without having a panel discussion or democratic vote that she would be the Queen Bee in charge of all of Sunshine's pill taking.

Not that Sunshine had a choice in the matter...even if she had said no, Queen was determined to grind the pills to powder dust and sprinkle them into Sunshine's daily glass of orange juice. The thought of outsmarting Sunshine with a glass of OJ sent Queen into a simultaneous laughing and coughing spell until Sunshine shot her the "You're embarrassing me, grandma," look that teenagers spend their years perfecting.

"Ok, Dr. Chung, you mentioned two surprises, please continue," Sunshine pleaded.

"Well, with your continued pill maintenance, I have decided that you are back to yourself enough to continue treatment on an outpatient basis from your home."

The news almost took Sunshine's breath away, and her immediate response was a loud shriek that could be heard almost to the end of the hallway. Instantly, her mind started spinning as she thought about all the college activities and assignments she had missed during her prolonged stay in the hospital.

"Dr. Chung, I've been locked away in this psych ward for a month waiting on someone who doesn't know much about me to say that I'm back to myself and give me permission to return to my temporarily suspended life. In your professional opinion, how did I get here in the first place?"

Dr. Chung cleared his throat as he carefully explained once again, "Sunshine, you had an episodic breakdown during finals and ended up in the hospital."

"No, Dr. Chung, I already know that part. Here is what I'm really asking…out of several thousand students at my school, how did this calamity happen to me?"

Sensing the emotional tug-of-war going on inside of Sunshine, Dr. Chung closed his charts and looked up to the ceiling as if the words of encouragement he needed were encased in the cracks on the wall. He continued, "Sunshine, mental illness does not discriminate. It knows no bounds or barriers. It crosses all gender, racial and economic boundaries. Now that it has touched your life, it will be your lifelong task to learn how to operate within this illness. It will be your life's journey to find a way to live your best life. Remember, medicine only works if you take it." And with that sage advice, Dr. Chung walked out of the room and left Sunshine with her precious family and her wildly scattered thoughts.

Sunshine sat on her hospital bed in a state of momentary disbelief and yet somewhat exhilarated that she would be leaving the hospital soon and picking her life back up. Although excited to be going home, she was still full of questions that not even her smarty-pants doctor seemed to be able to answer.

Looking toward the door, Sunshine blurted out her final thoughts to the doctor who was long gone. "Doc, all I want to know is, if I have to skip through life with a bag of pills by my side, how in the world can I become myself by swallowing a pill that is designed to change myself?"

Sensing that Dr. Chung was spending valuable moments with the next patient or perhaps off to lunch and completely out of earshot, Sunshine made up her mind that she would absolutely do and say anything to go home and get as far away from the hospital as possible. As she turned her gaze from the door toward the face of her grandmother, Sunshine wanted more than anything to share the fears bouncing around in her head that there was nothing left in her to love.

I want to scream. I am moments from being released from the hospital and yet I feel like my head is merely an empty projectile with just a few birds flying around in the dark.

She didn't say a word to express any of the anxiety, torment, joy, fear and butterflies that she was feeling; she simply longed to be held and squeezed tight. Queen knew what pain felt like and so she grabbed her granddaughter and stuffed her into her bosom as she quietly whispered in her ear, "Baby, there's always something left to love inside of everybody."

The most important part of the body ain't the heart
or the lungs or the brain. The biggest,
most important part of the body is the part that hurts.
Sekou Sundiata

CHAPTER 5

Embrace Your Crazy

What you say to yourself will determine your destiny.

Dear Diary...

It's been an entire year since I left my beloved university and the life that I once knew.

This right here hurts.

It hurts a lot!

Please don't ask me where it hurts. My answer would be it hurts everywhere if I was challenged to find the X that marks the spot.

My head hurts.

My eyes hurt.

My lower back hurts.

The pain finds a way to travel throughout my entire body all the way down to my toes.

There is pain in every inch of this new body that I've been living in since my breakdown.

Even my heart doesn't seem to beat the same.

*The simple fact is...I never thought I would be **"here."***

As she stared at the word "here," Sunshine was frozen in her thoughts as she contemplated its meaning. Life around her had gone on in its usual fashion from the very day of her episode. Campus life was bustling as the school calendar was packed with social events and continuous term paper deadlines. And yet, Sunshine was stuck "here" in her childhood bedroom, at the guidepost of her little life trying to get back to herself.

On the other hand, Sunshine was conflicted as to whether "here" really meant the struggle to find out where her "self" or "sanity" had gone off to and the battle to put "self" back in its rightful place. Sunshine knew it sounded crazy and was therefore reluctant to share her thoughts with anyone. She certainly didn't want to spend an extra minute going back and forth to the "hospital of last resort" where you go to put your broken self-back together again.

But the burning question that had Sunshine in a complete kerfuffle was, *Why won't anybody look me in the eye? It seems like ever since my breakdown, nobody takes the time to look at me anymore. At the hospital, the doctors would all come in the room with their eyes glued to their charts, scribbling notes as if my mortal body had shrunk to fit between the lines. Even my friends and family members would stop by the hospital and have the most challenging time figuring out what to do with their eyes. They would stare at the television intently or even scale the walls with their eyeballs. I would follow their gaze up the wall trying to discover what was so fascinating about the lime green walls. If the walls were so enthralling, wouldn't the vibrant color scheme be the go-to palette for our homes across the land? Or were the lime green walls the most available thing, anything to keep from looking at me?*

Sunshine wanted to scream at all the well-wishers and handlers that came to offer her comfort or healthcare. She wanted everyone to feel her frustration and understand that *anybody can look at you; the hardest challenge in life is finding someone that can see the same awesome rainbow that you see.* Yet, the raw truth was that most of the time, even she did not see beautiful rainbows with all their brilliant array of colors. The majority of days Sunshine spent her time locked in her room in a cocoon of silence and darkness, unable to express to anyone on the outside the torment that she was experiencing.

Sunshine felt that the burning question on everyone's mind was, "Do you feel like you're getting better?" It seemed like everyone wanted to be fed the perfect little comeback story - sickness to healing, weakness to strength, darkness to light and perhaps even broken to whole. Honestly, Sunshine felt like her entire body was patched back together with a little silly putty and a smidge of Elmer's glue.

The most awkward part was trying to find the words to describe the hurt and pain that was enveloping her whole being. Sunshine often imagined discovering a language composed solely of pain experiences that she could translate into ordinary words. She wanted to capture the pain and interpret its essence into the physical realm where it could be seen and smelled and caressed. Then she could reach out and kill it with her bare hands. Yes, destroy the thing that was eating away at her and robbing her of her mind.

Bursting through the walls of Sunshine's room, where she insulated herself from the outside world, was a noise that sounded like her grandmother wailing. As she listened rather intently, the noise articulated into words: "What on earth is that child doing up there in that room?" Although Sunshine continued to lick her wounds and feel sorry for herself, the door to her room and private sanctuary swung open, and her grandmother filled the doorway. She had long ago developed the characteristic swiftness to her gait when she was about to lay down the law. With an old-school look of disgust mixed with discernment on her face, Queen declared, "Baby, you gonna stop all that foot stomping on my floors today."

The foot stomping had become incessant over the last couple of months since Sunshine had come home from the hospital with her bag of magic pills. Queen had put on a brave face and swept into action and remained by Sunshine's hospital bedside until her release date. But the foot stomping that developed once Sunshine came home was on a whole other level. Although Queen had enough of the noise coming from Sunshine's room, it was still hard for her to believe that her sweet baby could possibly be hearing voices. Reluctantly, Queen began to find comfort in describing the voices in her granddaughter's head as birds the way Sunshine did, to ease the pain and constant worry about the changes that were happening inside of her.

Birds were something that Queen was very familiar with. Growing up a country girl in the deep south, Queen didn't have much in her arsenal to battle invisible voices talking to a person at all times of the day other than her tea leaves, ointments and a strong dose of prayer. But Queen knew for a fact that she had experience with loud, clucking birds that cluttered her childhood memory. From the time she was about five years old, she could remember running around the yard trying to corner the chosen bird for the evening dinner meal. Queen felt confident that if she didn't know much else, she knew how to catch birds. And eat them!

Queen went into a coughing spell that hurt her chest as she chuckled at the thought that the biggest birds she had ever caught turned out to be the two turkeys that eventually became her deceased husbands. And just like birds do, they would fly away for a few days or weeks when things got tough or the weather turned cold. Now, Queen remained unmovable in her belief that with the power of prayer, shooing the birds away from her granddaughter's mind would be just about as easy as killing and eating one. Or so she thought.

"One thing is for certain," Queen mumbled to herself as she pushed open the door as far as possible, "you gonna stop all that foot stomping up in this house. Today is the last day for that foot banging you carrying on with. I mean that!"

The foot stomping and tapping was getting louder and louder each day, and it was driving Queen up a wall. Standing in Sunshine's doorway, Queen shouted at the top of her lungs, "Devil, you can't stay here! Baby, you're going with me to see the doctor today. You won't be stomping your feet and banging on the walls not another night, if I got anything to do with it."

Queen didn't have the heart to plunge Sunshine any further into the type of storm that she was experiencing, even though she knew that Sunshine was not purposefully dragging the whole family through her own nightmare. As Queen moved further into the room to embrace her granddaughter, Sunshine leaned back just slightly out of reach. Sunshine was convinced she was crazy and there was nothing anyone could do about it, not even with hugs.

"Crazy almost felt good and somewhat normal," Sunshine sighed to herself as she hesitantly allowed her grandmother to embrace her in a full-frontal hug. Crazy was all that Sunshine had known for the last twelve months and it slowly but steadily felt like her new residence and resting place.

Later that evening, she reluctantly attended her bi-monthly group therapy session with strangers who were either depressed, hearing voices or bipolar. Sunshine sat completely still and remained silent, hoping that no one would recognize her or call on her to share her inner thoughts or feelings regarding her foot stomping escapades.

Everything was working as planned and Sunshine soon felt like the motivational speeches of "just say no to drugs" were coming to an end and the coast would finally become clear for her to find the fastest path to the exit door. Sunshine was absolutely relishing the fact that waiting on her Uber ride home was practically all that was left to do, when suddenly a patient from the group session pulled her to the side and announced, "I've been watching you for the entire meeting."

Sunshine deliberately gave him the side-eye to alert him to go talk to someone that cared. He stubbornly continued, "I felt the need to share with you the urgent message that you will never get out of these silly meetings and your dark hole if you continue your journey as uptight as you are."

"Let me tell you a little secret," the stranger ranted on, "in order to find joy in the person and the place in your life that you will eventually identify as your new self, you must embrace all of you, including your broken mind. **Somehow, you must find a way to celebrate the uniqueness that is you.**

"Please allow me to introduce myself, my name is Jordan Meadows. I am not new to this life nor am I only mentally ill. In fact, I was told to go home two years ago, but I refused."

Although Sunshine was not paying that much attention to Jordan's elaborate story, she was listening just enough to curiously blurt out, "Why would you do something so crazy as refuse to go home?"

Horrified, Sunshine clamped her mouth shut, but it was too late. She had accidently said the "C" word out loud. The look on her face clearly showed her frustration in the moment and she became flushed with embarrassment.

"Young lady, you must be new to this life?" Jordan inquired quizzically. "Let me tell you something, I've been called crazy all my life. From the time I started school, I've been riding the short bus. Can I let you in on a little secret? Most of the time, I am terrified of needles and start to shudder even before the nurses turn toward me with their secret weapon. Finally, after a lot of trial and error, we hit the jackpot in my roller coaster ride with mental illness through a drug called the Decanoid shot. My sweet back is the secret location on my body that the nurses selected to send the juice of the drug into my bloodstream. The shot lasted roughly thirty days, sort of a slow IV drip, and I pretty much went about life with the able assistance of my invisible friend. For the most part, a scarred-up butt was the only casualty of the sweet back shot," Jordan laughed to himself.

He slowly continued, "I've been here so long that I feel like everyone in this hospital is family, even while I am considered an institutionalized casualty. The daily structure and grind of psychiatric hospital life no longer feels like a struggle. In a strange kind of way, it feels good to be told what to do...

Get up.

Count time.

Eat breakfast.

Count time.

Eat dinner.

Count time.

Bed time.

Count time.

And repeat.

"The people in the white coats allowed me supervised visits home with my family from time to time, but it never felt quite right. If I left a room and did not return within a limited time, certain family members would come looking for me with dispatch. Once I was found, they would pepper me with questions like, 'are you ok? Do you need help?'

"And sometimes my family even had the nerve to outright cut my visit short by asking if I was ready to get back home. The simple truth is, I felt like a golden egg that nobody around me wanted to accidentally drop on their watch. It's as if the family consensus consisted of, *'Let's get this visit over with and get Jordan back to his hospital birdcage and allow his real handlers with the white jackets to protect him from himself.'*

"The real joke in my mind stemmed from all the violence and hatred that I was exposed to whenever I left the sanctuary and safety of the hospital. I was periodically sent home for forty-eight hours to my family that was too busy to love me. My disability, or perhaps insanity, seemed too uncomfortable and time-consuming for my immediate family to deal with. I soon found myself spending countless hours in a room that seemed to get smaller from all of my dark thoughts. All of this extra thinking only allowed time to drip by ever so slowly, while my family and friends were almost within arm's reach. I also started to feel that every time I was released to my family, there always seemed to be another act of violence being paraded across the evening news. I soon concluded that the real crazy people seem to be roaming the streets of the world outside my hospital doors."

"Let me tell you," Jordan exhaustively continued, "I ultimately became terrified of entering the outside world for short visits because of all the really crazy people that I encountered every time I was granted a weekend pass. When my time was up according to my health plan and time in the system, I weighed the odds of the least likely place that I could be killed by gun violence and the best place where I could find love. Both times the answer and the arch of safety became the psychiatric hospital.

"Call me crazy as much as you want, but gone are the days when you can challenge a guy in class to a fist fight at the ringing of the school bell. I may be housed with any number of school shooters that are populating our hospitals, but at least fist fighting is mostly all we can do. When I weighed the option of where I could find love, that was a little harder to choose," Jordan continued. "With a moment of clarity I realized that most of the nursing staff would love to stick me with needles at any given opportunity. The nurse techs would love to strap me down in a chair for countless hours or leave me in a padded room without a blanket for various rule infractions. This crazy love affair between patient and staff was the tipping point in my decision. For the past two years I have refused to go home to the world outside of this hospital because in my mind, beyond these walls is where the real crazy people live."

"Wow," was the first word that Sunshine found to utter. *What a long and never-ending story*, was all she could think as she smiled profusely to try and mask her unadulterated feelings. Jordan's decision to voluntarily stay in a mental hospital was the craziest thing she had heard in her entire young life. She wanted to yell, "Are you really that crazy?" But seeing how they both had patient wristbands on, crazy was only the start of their problems.

"Lord, help me to figure a way to quiet the noises in my head and somehow find joy in my circumstances," was all Sunshine could whisper as she climbed into the Uber for the ride home after therapy class. She longed for the solitude of her dorm room where she could curl up in the dark to try and figure out her ultimate escape plan from the voices twirling around in her head.

CHAPTER 6
Family First

A hard head makes a soft behind.

Dear Diary...

Asking the same question, "How did I get here?" over and over would at some point perhaps cross the line of crazy even for a crazy person, right? To answer my own question, I got here because I stopped taking my medication as prescribed. Although I thought it was funny and slick that I was off my meds, everyone that wished the best for me thought I was taking my pills like clockwork. Even my grandmother would stand like a watchdog as she handed the pill to me that would one way or another help to "bring me back to myself." Somehow, I had pushed past reality and was now precariously perched on the ledge of my very own secret society.

What's my secret? I would gladly grab the pill from my grandmother and throw it to the back of my throat. I'd reach for the water to send the pill on a mission to destroy the new me and return me to my old self. With a little practice I learned how to kick the pill forward from the labyrinth of its mission and hide the presumed scud missile under my tongue. All while making large gulping noises to satisfy my grandmother's hopes that the pill was on its way working for my good.

I won. Again. I would tell myself over and over that I won each time I was able to keep the magic pills out of my bloodstream. As much as I try to think of all the worst case scenarios, I'm sure I will not be ready for any sudden implosion that may hit my fragile young life.

With all of that extra winning going on in my mind, I still managed to convince myself that destruction on some level was headed my way due to my ability to perform pill acrobatics. In my limited knowledge of science, I knew that I didn't want to feel depressed and I definitely want the voices to stop. Yes, the voices would eventually stop each time I kept the pills coming down the pipeline…but at what cost? Everything the doctors tried in their attempt to fix my broken mind, I slowly and reluctantly felt the end result was that I became a casualty. Either I would sleep up to fifteen hours a day or I would be in such a lethargic state that I could easily be compared to a walking zombie.

When I decided to deceive my grandmother and everyone that loved me by not taking my prescribed medication, I couldn't see beyond the pain and the mess of my current situation. In my mind, my rainbow was being blocked by the trees in my forest.

As smart as Sunshine thought she was, she found herself back in the hospital, thanks to her bright idea and belief that not taking her medication would be the best treatment method to make her well. She had checked her wild thoughts with no one. In complete desperation regarding her situation, Sunshine's ill-conceived decision culminated in her fourth visit to the hospital in the last year. It was slowly becoming her new normal. College life, boyfriends and her first job seemed light years away from her reality of today as she struggled to keep her thoughts from running together in congested sentences that never ended. Ironically, as Sunshine fought to remember her whereabouts, she was desperately trying not to think about the fact that she was actually sitting on her hospital bed, which was really a form of thinking about it.

Sunshine grabbed one of the magazines that the church mothers dropped off on their weekly rounds of visiting the sick, but her mind would read the words and somehow circle back and reread the same paragraph over and over again in complete despair. In fact, she did everything she could to keep her imagined reality just the way she perceived it in her head by forcing her eyes shut as tightly as she could for hours at a time. As irrational as it sounded, she felt that if she could somehow keep her eyes closed, perhaps she could remain in the safety of her bedroom and the comfort of her little world.

Not so. Once dispatched to the hospital for a "touch up," as Sunshine called her visits, all avenues of privacy were thrown out the window and she somehow became a willing participant in the roller coaster ride that was her hospital stay. As if to prove this point, without even a courtesy knock or request to enter, Nurse Hilda came bursting through the door and into Sunshine's private mind bubble pity party. She had the audacity to march straight to the window and pull the curtains open to welcome in the sunlight of a new day which deliberately pierced through Sunshine's closed eyelids.

How on earth did I get so lucky to have such an overzealous bed czar who never misses a day from work, thought Sunshine. "Please, please not today," she whispered under her breath as she scurried to dive deeper under her blankets.

"You know I heard that," Nurse Hilda responded. "Baby, not on my watch," she asserted as she ripped the covers from her slothful sleeping angel. She continued her onslaught. "You will not sleep your life away while I'm on duty here at this hospital. I have told you a thousand times, if you work the program, the program will work for you, but you must be willing to do the work."

Sunshine had heard these fancy clichés countless times before and she wanted no part of the programs or group sessions where everyone would dig deep and explore their inner feelings.

What Sunshine longed for and only imagined in her secret world was the good times of her brief college experience and how simple life was somewhere in her past where she had accidentally misplaced herself. Knowing that she would never be able to squeeze her body into her past or the place that her mind so frequently drifted to, Sunshine decided to confide in her nurse with one of her crazy thoughts. Simply because Hilda was making it her duty on earth to torment her, Sunshine felt that it was only fair to give her nurse's brain a homework assignment.

"Excuse me, Nurse Hilda." Sunshine cautiously proceeded with the thought that had been floating around in her head for some time, hoping that she had chosen the right person to disclose her insides to. "Could you please help me understand why it is so easy for me to fall asleep and connect my dreams to my perceived reality, and I can wake up and somehow go about my life making my dreams come true? Is there any chance that I could take this thing called schizophrenia and attach the voices in my head to a dream and allow this odd reality to branch off and become a separate delusional entity apart from me and free me of this monster?"

Nurse Hilda stood motionless, confounded for the first time in her twenty years of medical service by such a brilliant assessment of logic and reason. Unable to move her mouth quickly enough to catch up to the brain surges going on in her mind in reaction to such a peculiar question, she was relieved by the large amount of hubbub and noise going on outside of Sunshine's hospital room.

"What on earth is all that noise?" Hilda mumbled to herself. Moving toward the door in search of the reason for all the commotion, she was secretly hoping that the distraction on the outside of the door would somehow be the thing to deflect from having to answer the question bouncing off the walls in the room.

"It's him. It's him. I can't believe it's him!"

As Hilda peered out of the door she quickly located a group of patients standing around a young man as he was signing autographs at the nurse's station. *Well, I will put a stop to this disturbance immediately,* she thought as she walked with vigor toward the unauthorized, vibrant crowd. "Young man, I am the head nurse in charge of this floor and I do not allow any rambunctiousness on my watch. How can I help you?"

Looking somewhat bewildered by the aggressive spirit of the lady with a hospital badge, Lil Son smartly decided to diffuse the situation by clearing his throat and slowly releasing his megawatt smile. "My name is Lil Son and I am looking for my baby sister Sunshine Black." He opened his mouth just enough to display all of his beautiful pearly whites in Hilda's direction and immediately melted all the annoyance that she had brought with her to the nurse's station. Somehow, with all of the many stories told by Sunshine regarding the wild success of her brother in the music industry since his crossover from gospel to mainstream, Hilda was completely puzzled as to why she had never mentioned his lovely teeth.

Forcing her way out of the matrix that a person with a beautiful Hollywood smile can command, Hilda gathered her thoughts as she moved closer to Lil Son and his mesmerizing smile. "Hello, my name is Hilda and I am your sister's personal nurse," she cooed while smiling uncontrollably.

"Sunshine is a delightful patient and I get nothing but joy coming to work and taking care of her needs. Please follow me," she continued disappointedly as she noticed that Lil Son was reading and responding to his text messages and not overtly enamored by her pretty green eyes. As they approached the room, Hilda opened the door and then instinctively headed in the opposite direction. Lil Son stood in the doorway as he finished up a text to his publicist: JUST TELL THEM HE'S ON HIS WAY TO REHAB! *How could this be happening to me,* he thought. *Just when the biggest song of my career could possibly be recorded by the biggest pop star in the industry, he decides to land on TMZ for his proclivity for bad behavior. I must find the right star power to record my song, Loving You Again.*

After sending two more texts regarding his search for a singer, Lil Son finally entered the hospital room and hurriedly moved toward Sunshine's bedside until a familiar voice stopped him in his tracks.

"Where have you been?" Sunshine yelled.

"Lil Sis, it's me, your brother. Aren't you glad to see me?" Lil Son was completely caught off guard by his sister's sour welcome. With so much on his plate, Lil Son wisely chose not to respond to the verbal tirade being hurled in his direction. Instead, he quickly extended his arm and revealed what he was hiding behind his back. "I brought you some flowers."

Sunshine took a cursory glance at the flowers and briefly weighed them against the pain she felt in her heart by not having her brother at her side as she faced the storm of mental illness showing up in her life. Somehow, the flowers became light as a feather once she placed them on her imaginary scale to see what level of positivity she should approach this unresolved family situation with.

"Well, I haven't seen or heard from you in over a year," Sunshine finally declared. "You gonna march in here with a handful of almost dead roses as if you just got back from the corner store with some ice cream and a bag of chips?"

"But...let me explain," Lil Son tried to interject.

However, Sunshine was having none of it and had saved just enough of her sanity on this day for the showdown by her bedside. "And just to be clear," she exhaled deeply, "please leave your Grammy awards and BET trophies at the door. They cannot provide me any hugs or pump any love into my life. In fact, I believe they are the objects that stole you away from me."

After her brief but necessary outburst, Sunshine's heart opened up ever so slightly due to her love for her brother. As the tears started to slowly flow down her face, Sunshine struggled to contain her sobbing as she leaned forward into the safety of her brother's outstretched arms. The moment was bittersweet as they held each other and allowed the silence to bring them up to date regarding his unexplained absence.

With renewed resolve, Sunshine wiped the tears from her face. She dug deep into her soul and soon found her voice once again. Closing her eyes and taking another deep breath to gather her strength, she looked into her brother's eyes and asked the question resonating in her heart. "Why did you leave me? Was I not worth more than the fame you discovered?"

Lil Son inhaled as much oxygen as he could into his lungs while searching for the words to explain his absence from the lives of his family. He had known for several years that the day would one day come where he would have to explain his highbrow Hollywood ways, and he somehow felt that today would be the day as he squeezed his sister's hand.

Hesitantly, Lil Son found his voice. "I foolishly thought everything would remain the same as I hopped aboard a rocket ship with no pilot. With no available directions to help me navigate my sudden trajectory into fame, I just went along for the ride of a lifetime." Over the next hour, Lil Son allowed his truth to pour out as he shared how his dreams to make music and a little money quickly turned into more than he could ever imagine. The accolades poured in regarding his gift and it had satisfied his burgeoning ego, but deep down inside he had already known he was extremely gifted.

"The simple fact is that the Grammy awards came way too quick in my career," Lil Son finally acknowledged. "Incredibly, after only one song and no booking agent, I suddenly began the rocket ride of my life. My phone would ring nonstop from some of the biggest stars in the world to write radio-ready songs and the money they threw at me was intoxicating. I was a church boy writing songs for pop stars and no one cared as long as the hits kept coming. The pressure to stay relevant became harder than my original drive to be famous. I soon lost focus of the ones that loved me, like you and Queen, before any of the awards shows and radio spins showed up in my life."

As they continued to hold hands, Sunshine reached over to wipe the tears from her brother's eyes as she slowly grasped that his words came from the safe place of his heart that often provided her a sense of security during her childhood. Sunshine realized that she felt her brother's incredible pain and the loneliness he must have endured as he became famous and discovered his handlers and friends in his circle were all strangers.

Looking into his eyes, Sunshine leaned over and whispered in his ear, "You do know it would have been easier if I traded my nightmare of living with schizophrenia for your wild dream of fame and went with you for the ride?"

They shared their very first laugh of the visit, but Sunshine quickly returned the mood solemn as she realized her best friend was finally home and an unsuspecting victim to listen to the ramblings of her mind. "Lil Son, there are about a hundred billion stars in our vast Milky Way, which would account for about one for every person who ever lived," Sunshine continued as she searched for her words. "With all the technology and weapons that we have on this planet, why is it that we can't realign or remove any stars out of the universe?" She reluctantly released his hand as she attempted to describe the pain she felt on the inside of her body. "That's how weird it feels to be me and know you're crazy and not be able to do anything about it."

Sunshine looked into her brother's face while she searched for any small glimmer in his eyes that had allowed her to feel safe in his presence as a little girl before he left for college some ten years earlier. Unable to decipher the look on his face, Sunshine decided to hurl caution to the wind and opened up to her brother in a way that would cause her counselors and program facilitators to applaud her for such deep thought.

She looked at Lil Son for help as she fought to find the words to heal her aching heart. She touched his shoulder ever so slightly as she guardedly asked, "Why is it ok to reach out and grab a pill to mend a broken heart, but if your brain is malfunctioning and in need of some extra help, people are ashamed to grab a pill to fix and heal the situation? Why must one be forced to feel shame and live a life of secret for a broken mind and not a broken heart? It's not like you believe yourself to be normal like everyone else. Inside your deepest inside you know that there is a problem. But you just can't figure out a way to fix it and break through to the other side where normal people reside."

"I know an easy fix for your conundrum," Nurse Hilda announced as she reappeared in the room and slid herself into their A and B conversation. "Sunshine, have you been taking your meds?" Lil Son turned away from Hilda to face his sister, hoping her answer would satisfy his curiosity regarding her treatment plan.

Although she initially ignored Hilda's question since it felt like the entire medical staff knew she was back in the hospital for not taking her meds, it quite frankly felt like she was under attack by an undercover agent of the government on loan to the hospital. After a few moments of silence, Sunshine finally responded, "None of them have the right effect on my mind."

"Correction! None of them have worked effectively, yet," Nurse Hilda interjected rather harshly.

At that moment, Dr. Chung, who had been on the other side of the room tending to another patient and writing in his charts, finally finished his assessment and quietly headed for the door. Abruptly, Sunshine, seeing her moment passing away, shouted out to her physician. "Dr. Chung, what can I do to help myself?"

Her physician slowly turned around to face his young patient while gathering his thoughts. He took his time as he searched for the words to encourage Sunshine. He pondered for a moment as though he was peeling his thoughts from off the ceiling. Then, he finally shared, "You must take your medicine as prescribed. You must follow the treatment plan for it to be effective. And, most importantly, Sunshine, you must allow the passing of time to do its healing work."

He turned to Nurse Hilda as he gave his order that he wanted to see Sunshine again in seven days. Although he was not technically talking to Sunshine, she surmised, *you can kind of measure your level of crazy based on how soon the professionals want to see you again.* She half-heartedly chuckled, "Last year when I first arrived at the hospital, the medical staff wanted to see me every day, now it's only once a week."

Dr. Chung approached the door to continue his daily rounds of patient visitation. Sunshine wanted to say thank you, but her mind was all over the place with countless thoughts. As he closed the door, Dr. Chung looked over his shoulder and smiled at Lil Son as he reminded his patient to "keep God first and surround yourself with love from family and friends." He also left her with a little drip of hope as he declared, "Sunshine, you must do the work, but somehow you will survive this storm and one day help others."

CHAPTER 7
Don't Move My Mountain

Dear Diary...

It seems like life is back to my adjusted new normal. I found myself in the hospital for another touch up because I once again had stopped taking my meds. I have no idea why I would sabotage my very own recovery process, but every time I start feeling "back to myself" I question the need for that pesky little pill. And then I stop taking it.

"I got this!"

I'm really good for a spell and somehow I find a way to operate at a very high level in the real world. I answer questions appropriately and seem adjusted enough to fit in most social settings without any radical adjustments. And then without any warning that I can properly acknowledge, I rudely crash. Hard.

Deep down in my insides I know that I must push past the silly

birds that I allow to dance around in my head. Yes, I am learn-
ing that I must fight through the unannounced circumstances
that show up in my life. Somehow, I realize the secret answer
is that I must find the strength to break free of this mental
bondage. But each time I face adversity in my day to day life,
I seem to crumble under the pressure.

As much as I love rainbows in the sky and sitting in my room
by the windowsill, it's been hard for me to see beyond the
window seat view of my broken mind.

"And that is exactly why you're back in the hospital. Same floor, different bed!" The voices in Sunshine's head shouted at her in a familiar, bombastic tone as their unified laughter reverberated throughout her body. Sunshine repeatedly thought she was done with the psychotic voices having a party in her head at all times of the day or night. Then, the voices would find a way to flare up and create a dust storm in her young life without so much as a "please." It took a long time and several trips to the hospital to get it through her thick skull that the voices mostly arrived whenever she stopped taking her meds. Sunshine absolutely hated the rigid regimen of pill management and the awful thought of doing anything twice a day for the rest of her life. But, she eventually found out by trial and foolish error that she hated going to the hospital even more.

"Ok, I will go," Sunshine blurted out to her nurse without any warning.

"Go where, child?" Nurse Hilda responded as she slowly shook herself free from the mental countdown of the last forty minutes before her twelve-hour shift ended.

"I'm ready to go wherever I must go to rid myself of this pain that afflicts my mind," Sunshine confirmed. "I'm finally ready to follow the program so I can find peace in my life and hopefully begin to put the pieces of my young life back together again."

Nurse Hilda could not believe her ears even though she was an eyewitness to the many roadblocks and failed attempts a patient could take to reach the place where they became sick and tired of the roller coaster ride. Each announcement from a patient admitting an attitude change toward complete surrender to the process of living with a mental illness brought tears to her eyes.

She reached toward Sunshine's hand to offer comfort as she tried to hide the tears that were suddenly blurring her vision. Hesitantly, Hilda asked, "Are you sure you're ready for this new journey?" The look that Sunshine gave her nurse reassured her that no storm or mountain would be big enough to keep her from finding the joy of living her best life.

Later that same evening, Sunshine found herself in her group therapy session where outpatients of the psychiatric hospital were matched with professional people in the community struggling with the same issues. The stated purpose of the class was to show the patients there was no specific face to mental illness or depression. The medical staff of the hospital wanted to impart the fact that mental illness affects all genders, races, socio-economic classes and professions.

As the class got under way, everyone in attendance introduced themselves. The first person to speak was a slightly balding middle-aged man named Jose. He had come to the class to learn how to quiet the suicidal thoughts he had been having since the breakup with his girlfriend and the loss of his job. Sunshine sat there desperately trying to listen to Jose's struggles to place a Band-Aid on his pain, all the while hoping to find the secret matrix code to her own personal dilemma. Yet, all she could think about in the moment was how easily the answers came to her regarding fixing the lives of her fellow group members.

Sunshine unapologetically blurted out, "I got it!" as everyone in the small group setting turned toward her. But once she saw all the eyeballs staring fiercely in her direction, Sunshine decided to keep her genius idea a secret. She sheepishly replied "never mind" as she feverishly hoped that the annoying eyes would find something else to focus on. In spite of this small faux pas, Sunshine allowed a tiny smile to paint her face, adamant in her own mind that the answer to Jose's problem would be to just find another girlfriend and job. Problem solved.

Sunshine continued to use all of her strength to focus on the kumbaya therapy session that was supposed to magically change her life. As she listened intently to the stories and cries for help, she had an epiphany. Stunned, she concluded with absolute amazement that there must be an outstanding amount of people in life who were messed up in the head. *And to think, during this sometimes frightening journey through mental illness, I foolishly thought I was the only crazy person in the whole world,* she mused.

The next speaker who had the temerity to share his personal issues referred to himself as Alfred. He spoke about how he grew up in foster care all his life and how the experience led him on the path to obtain a master's degree in Counseling to help others. Alfred opened up to the group and shared his fears of abandonment and how it crippled his every attempt at fixing his own insecurities in his quest to find love.

"Welcome to the club, buddy," Sunshine gushed under her breath as she moved her hands up to her mouth to contain her sudden outburst. After another hour of this love fest and collective soul searching, it soon became evident that everyone was waiting on a particular individual who had not said a single word. With bated breath, everyone looked forward to the moment when the out-of-place guest would finally open her mouth and justify her presence. The silence bounced off the walls and echoed the same message that everyone in the room wanted to ask…"You do know you're at a therapy session for people messed up in the head?" The collective consensus of the group seemed to be, "We already know who you are, we just want to know, why are you here?"

Slowly, almost as if on cue, the mystery guest cleared her throat and decided it was time to live a life free from her debilitating secret. "Hi, my name is Raelyn and being here today is the hardest thing I've ever done. You may be looking at a woman who is heralded around the world for her voice, but I am here because I have hit my personal rock bottom. I've done everything in my career to ignore the fact that I suffer from anxiety and depression and for years, I was afraid to tell anyone about my condition. The mental paralysis of having my secret exposed and ultimately not being loved by others kept me from seeking help. I didn't want to appear different, so I took up my cross and suffered in silence with bouts of depression. As crazy as this may sound, the truth is that I went through life singing to people all over the world to make them feel happy while I grieved quietly on the inside with my own debilitating pain."

Counselor Marybeth, who was leading the group session, persuaded Raelyn to continue in her healing by encouraging, "Tell us how this pain made you feel." "Yes, go deeper," the youngest patient in the group, T-Mack, cooed. He gleefully salivated at the insane idea that he was crazy enough in the head to be in the same messed up group session as one of the biggest gospel artists of his generation.

Raelyn quickly shot T-Mack a reprimanding side-eye before opening her heart through the portal of her pain. She continued, "I tried desperately to share with those closest to me that it was getting harder and harder to get up and sing in front of others while I felt so broken on the inside. Everyone kept telling me that the show must go on. I was the 'show' and it didn't seem to matter much that I was broken and in need of repair and rest. The saddest part of my struggle always came after leaving the stage and the roaring accolades of the crowd and coming home to an empty house. The applause made me feel loved until I turned the doorknob on my home and found only silence. As I traveled the world and suffered in my own little world with depression, I came to realize that people giving advice to loved ones living with mental illness to snap out of it is like telling a deaf person to listen harder."

Looking back at T-Mack to make sure he had no further side comments, Raelyn decided to finish her story and simultaneously allow the pain in her heart to gently ooze out. She exhaled rather loudly and continued, "I pretty much suffered from anxiety and depression as far back as my memory can go, but for the majority of my adult life, my little secret seemed like a managed annoyance. It wasn't until I was discovered on my college campus and thrown into the world as the heir apparent to the late Mahalia Jackson did my illness flare up. I found myself singing in front of audiences around the world in venues that I could hardly pronounce. I knew I was gifted but deep down inside I longed to return to the days when I was just a local church singer with a very big voice.

"My biggest dream since I was a little girl was to sing in my daddy's church and maybe travel around to four or five nearby states as the top-secret weapon to warm the crowd up before he began to preach. I never desired anything more than my small dream and was completely unprepared when the spotlight of fame unlocked a world I never imagined or felt I could ever grow accustomed to. On the other hand, my mentor, producer and manager, Lil Son, seemed to embrace the fame and all the perks that it opened up to us. I came to see the spotlight as a vehicle to share the message of love to the world. My mentor soon became enamored by the glitter and started to become more like the world that we were sent to change.

"The more I was celebrated with applause and fame, the more the spotlight felt like a tightening noose around my neck to choke my mind away from my body. Eventually, I walked away from my record deal, the accolades and money. I was exhausted from all of the constant travel and simultaneously depressed from the emptiness that I felt on the inside. Today, I stand on the biggest stage of my life within this room as I shed my fears and debilitating pain and declare that I no longer have to carry this secret pain around any longer."

The room remained silent for about twenty seconds as Raelyn's awesome story stirred inside the hearts of everyone present. Then suddenly, Jordan blurted out the thoughts of many in the room. "Ain't no way I'm walking away from that much money. We would peacefully drive off into the sunset together in my new Lamborghini."

Once MaryBeth quieted the outburst and the silly laughter simmered down, it became apparent that everyone in the room had spoken. There was nothing left to do but sit still and weigh how much more messed up the other lives were than their own. Sunshine sank down into her chair and kept her eyes trained on the floor, trying desperately to hide in plain sight and hoping that no one would notice that she hadn't gone "deep fishing," as the testimonials were called. But her heart sank as Jordan interrupted the silence by declaring, "Hey, we can't leave yet, we haven't heard from my friend, Sunshine."

In a voice filled with caution, Sunshine hesitantly began, "I don't know much about anything regarding this thing called life…but…" Before she could expand her thought, Jordan interrupted and insisted in his enormous voice, "Certainly life has taught you something?"

Sunshine shifted her eyes toward Jordan to signal that their friendship would be in serious jeopardy with any further outburst. After a slight pause to gather herself and keep her train of thought away from strangling Jordan, Sunshine looked over at her counselor and then Raelyn. She found the strength through their eye contact to share a segment of the miracle that was taking place in her own small world. She slowly inhaled a deep breath of courage as she continued, **"I've learned that mountains don't move."**

"Well, dah! Tell us something we don't know, Sherlock," Jordan interjected.

Sunshine quickly snapped, "Just one more time, Jordan," as she shot him an icy stare down. That was finally enough for Jordan to quiet down, as he seemed to realize he was pretty close to the end of the rope with Sunshine.

Looking upward toward the ceiling as if somehow the strength needed to share her testimony was embedded in the crevices of the wall, Sunshine gained courage as she sensed the positive energy of the settled room.

Finally finding her voice again, she continued in a hushed tone. "Ever since I became sick during my freshman year in college, I expected God to immediately show up in my life and just move the mountains that I faced out of my path. The real truth is I was shocked and bewildered when I would wake up every morning and my mountain would still be precariously perched directly in the path I was carving out for myself. For the longest time I was willing to try anything to fix my mind except the task of climbing mountains. Going around my mountain always seemed like the best option rather than facing it and climbing its steep precipice one step at a time."

Sunshine continued, "The hard work of mountain climbing on this journey called mental illness just didn't seem fair when all my college friends were only constantly complaining about homework, term papers and relationships. But the longer I stayed at the base of my new mountain of circumstances, pretty much just mad at the basic requirements like pill management, I found that my mountain would grow more and more insurmountable each and every day.

"It was only when I changed my prayer and thought process and moved toward asking God to provide just enough watering posts and resting places along the journey that I gradually realized I would be ok. The more I viewed my problems through the lens of prayer and the complete surrender of the mountain moving process to the Creator, I slowly started noticing new resting places and watering holes where I could renew my strength along the way."

After sharing her testimony, Sunshine felt an enormous relief and looked around the room as each person affirmed her healing process with an approving smile. Finally, as the session ended and the room began to empty, Sunshine pressed her way to Raelyn until she was within earshot and able to shake her hand. But instead of grabbing her hand, Sunshine leaned toward her and summoned the courage to whisper into her ear, "I know you!"

The boldness of the declaration caught Raelyn by surprise. Even though she had bared her soul in the meeting to hopefully find relief from her complex life, Raelyn had no intention of exposing her deepest secret to anyone that really knew her. The plan was to expose her vulnerability and fears to complete strangers who would disappear just like they did when she left the stage and the closing curtains signaled the end of the show. Somehow, it had never dawned on Raelyn that there was the slim possibility that the one counseling session she had selected to fix her life would be the exact same class where someone from her past would be messed up enough in the head to also attend.

After taking a closer look at Sunshine's face, Raelyn gripped the back of her chair in an attempt to steady her balance as she realized exactly who the young lady was. She was unsure of her name, but knew with complete certainty who she was related to in the music industry. Instantly, powerful feelings of abandonment and disappointment came rushing to the forefront of her mind.

Raelyn quickly scanned the room in complete panic mode as she contemplated how on earth someone from her past could show up to the very same healing session. Once reassured that no one else from her past was lurking in the room, she finally pulled Sunshine close as she whispered, "What are you doing here?"

CHAPTER 8
Even Birds Can Sing

"A bird doesn't sing because it has an answer,
it sings because it has a song."
Maya Angelou

Dear Diary...

I'm going to be ok.

Sunshine had been sitting on her hospital bed for over an hour staring at the words, **"I'm going to be ok,"** trying to figure out what exactly that would mean for her young life. Each time, she drew a blank thought as she painfully tried to imagine what it would feel like to be "ok."

It was only after she heard a coughing noise did she look up and realize she was not alone, and found Chaplin Mullins sitting comfortably in a chair by the window.

"How are you feeling, Sunshine?" the pastor asked gently.

"I have no clue," Sunshine replied. "I'm just sick and tired of being sick. I wish there was some way I didn't have to go through this dark hole."

"All things work together for good in your life – even your illness. The book of James in the Bible tells us to count it all joy when we face trials. Sunshine, I can't wait to see what God is trying to teach you through this illness."

"Well, Pastor, I just hope that whatever God is trying to teach me, I will learn the lesson with extreme quickness," Sunshine responded.

"Here we go again," Sunshine quietly sighed a few hours later as the door to her room was abruptly flung open. She looked up from her bed and glanced at the face of a joyful Nurse Hilda bursting through the door in preparation mode, ready to dispense the morning dose of medication to affect her mood and quality of life.

"Must you be so happy to stick me with your magic needle every morning?" Sunshine asked in exasperation.

"Baby, this needle that I give you twice a day should really be the least of your worries," Hilda confided. As she leaned closer into Sunshine's personal space, she confidently whispered into her ear, "You got way bigger fish to fry than to be thinking about what kind of juices I'm sticking you with."

"What on earth could be more important?" Sunshine implored.

Nurse Hilda forcefully leaned all the way into Sunshine's presence, shattering her personal two feet rule as if she didn't want any parts of her words to miss her patient's defiant eardrum. "Baby, you have got to find a way to get out of here."

The statement shocked Sunshine and it took a moment for her to catch her breath. In actuality, no medical personnel had spoken to her in such a manner or had taken any special interest in her inner feelings during the course of her illness.

"You mean escape? Run away?" Sunshine quizzically replied.

"No, foolish girl!" Nurse Hilda scoffed. She continued, "You've got to find a way to quiet the noise and constant chatter in your head. There have been thousands of people before you, perhaps millions that have tried to kill the voices that have found comfort and a place of rest in the crevices of their mind. But, without continued professional help, you will become the sacrifice on the altar as you courageously, yet insanely take on the task of trying to slay the mystical birds flying around in your head."

"Let me be completely clear with you," Hilda explained as she shed all personal fear of getting too emotionally involved with her patient. "You ain't gonna ever get out of this hospital that some call the crazy house until you teach the birds in your head to sing a new song." And for the first time since Sunshine fell to the floor of her university cafeteria due to the banging noises in her head, someone was finally speaking a language that she could understand. With a sudden, renewed interest in life, Sunshine was intrigued that her nurse had found a way to get past her pain and knock on the doorstep of her inner soul. This new collision within her mind was intriguing and now Sunshine wanted to know more about this crazy escape plan.

With just a hint of hesitation, but fueled by the despairing realization that she was completely out of ideas regarding her own recovery, Sunshine propped herself up in bed. Excitedly she nodded her approval for Hilda to fully reveal the daring escape plan to her mental freedom. She anticipated with wide-eyed eagerness that her nurse and newly-minted friend would continue to direct her to some magic key. This key would somehow lead to the magic door that she could unlock in a desperate attempt to get out of the prison of the mind.

Sensing that she had finally deactivated the imaginary wall between staff and patient, Hilda resumed her stealth navigation to reach her new friend. "Sunshine, the biggest lie that mental illness screams at you is that you're finished, and you have nothing left to offer society. Let me tell you, your broken mind does not make you a broken person. Your real strength in life comes from inside of you. With a relentless pursuit, you must diminish the noise of your surroundings. You must find a way to get quiet enough to listen to your inner spirit and allow your Creator to birth in you a new song."

With the power of Nurse Hilda's words finally saturating Sunshine's mind and body, the two ladies instinctively reached out and embraced each other. This light embrace allowed the powerful vibration of faith to plant the seed in Sunshine the possibility that today could be the day she would begin the journey of walking through her storm with joy.

In reality, not much changed since the emotional locking and unlocking of their embrace. The medicine would still have to do its enchanted medical work. Although Sunshine was showing signs that the battle was being won, Nurse Hilda knew that the only change that really mattered would be the thought in Sunshine's mind that "I can do this."

"Everything else will be a work in progress," Hilda gently admonished Sunshine as she purposely wished for this new flame to stay lit inside her patient. She softly whispered in her ear, "I want you to know that the challenges of mental illness will still have moments of flare up in your life."

As the two ladies reluctantly released their embrace, Hilda held tight just a second longer as she shared the words that dropped in her spirit. **"Sunshine, the storms that rise up in your life are exactly where God is going to do His best work in your life.** Remember, there are people on the shores of life that are waiting on you to come through your storm with the good news of your testimony."

The ladies wiped their eyes and sealed their commitment to support each other as Sunshine slowly started to understand the burgeoning new chapter unfolding in her young life. Hilda methodically fixed her face ever so briefly before slipping out of the room and scurrying back to her nurse's station and the never-ending amount of charts and paperwork.

Missing Hilda by just mere minutes, Raelyn walked in the room oblivious to the lovefest that had just taken place between Sunshine and her favorite nurse. Approaching Sunshine's bed, she announced, "I wanted to stop by to thank you for sharing your struggles of living with mental illness during our last several sessions. I realize now that I must pray and continue to talk to my therapist in order to navigate through this journey called life."

As Sunshine leaned forward to embrace Raelyn, she suddenly remembered that they had never spoken about her brother Lil Son. Sunshine held back her desire to share the good news that he was in town for a few weeks and was currently on his way to the hospital for another visit. She didn't want to give Raelyn the chance to bolt and avoid seeing Lil Son. Instead, Sunshine just made small talk, hoping her mundane dribbles would keep her friend in the room long enough for her brother to show up.

"Raelyn, do you think you will ever sing again?" Sunshine sheepishly implored. As Raelyn considered the explosive question and all the little trap doors that could be attached to resuming her life as a singer, the door finally swung open and in the doorway stood Lil Son. Sunshine tried her best to keep her smile from covering her entire face as she triumphed in her accomplished mission. Raelyn, on the other hand, stood near the window frozen in shock from seeing her former music collaborator and mentor.

Lil Son stopped at the sight of his first love, stunned. "I thought I would never see you again," he finally managed.

"At least I said goodbye," Raelyn responded.

"Leaving is not a goodbye," Lil Son shot back rather coldly.

"Ok, this is not happening!" Sunshine shouted, desperate to change the mood in the room. The two former musical partners and lovers ignored the fact that anyone else was in the room as they continued to look into each other's eyes. Their gaze told most of the backstory as Lil Son wrestled with how to share the internal, one-sided conversations he'd had with her over the past ten years.

"You never gave our ending a chance at survival or a safe place to land," Lil Son finally spoke, breaking the cold silence permeating the room with words that he had covertly held for years. As the words fell off of his lips it brought a slight healing balm to the pain he felt for losing his best friend at the explosive start of his career. The loss had been very sudden and sharp, and the pain continued to play over and over in his mind for years after the separation.

Raelyn took what seemed like an eternity to completely turn around from the window and finally face the mentor that had helped launch her career straight out of college. Thoughts of gratitude rushed into her body and flooded her mind as she stood there looking at Lil Son. Determined not to cry, Raelyn found the courage to respond by simply asking, "Why didn't you come after me?"

Lil Son paused, because he really did not know how to answer the question. He maneuvered slightly away from the comfort of the open door where the path to his escape was clear. Almost in unison, Raelyn moved from the windowsill and sat on the edge of the bed where she could navigate a quiet exit and take her tears with her, if necessary. In his newly discovered territory by the window, Lil Son looked out onto the landscape for some help with the profound question… "Why didn't you come after me?"

Within moments, he noticed a bird sitting on a nearby ledge going about his daily bird duties completely oblivious to the fact that his antics were going to be the inspirational vitamin of the day. Lil Son noted with pleasure how freely the bird went about his activities. Turning from the window to face Raelyn, he instinctively decided to unleash the pain in his heart with the same fervor. "Raelyn," he began, "when we met on our college campus, you were like a little bird sitting on a pedestal just singing your little beak off because of the beautiful songs stored in your heart. I came along and heard your gift and became the melody to your song by figuring out how to share your incredible voice with the world."

He continued, "When the spotlight became too much and you walked away, it felt like I got caught up in the baggage of fame that you discarded as you returned to your old life. I knew we wanted different things in life but the applause and desire for fame kept me from understanding that your goodbye was not meant to include me."

"So, why didn't you go after her?" Sunshine interrupted the soap opera playing out in her room with her comment as she sensed that the showdown was getting butter-popcorn good. Slowly, Lil Son looked back out the window as he gathered the strength to answer the question that apparently refused to go away. Before speaking, he shot his little sister a scorching eye burner to remind her that flies on walls were not supposed to talk or interrupt. He turned back toward Raelyn and found the courage to open the cage to his broken heart. With a slight hesitation he fumbled his words but finally continued, "I didn't come after you because I didn't know how. I spent my whole life being chased by pastors, church leaders and wedding planners all wanting the best musician for their program or special event. With the fuel of people telling me I was gifted, I just felt that you would always be there. I lost touch with the importance of keeping good people around and when you decided to walk away, the fleeting fumes of fame became my only friend."

It had been years since their hit song, "My Friend," sizzled on the gospel charts and became a crossover hit. The former music duo had followed completely different life trajectories and lost contact. After Raelyn left the partnership, she quietly went back to a life of telling others about her friend Jesus and singing in churches that were much smaller than the symphony halls and concert venues of her former life as a gospel star. On the other hand, Lil Son chose to chase the temporary spotlight of fame and the adulation of his peers. Now he was finding that this endless desire to please others through his music and continuous string of hit songs was utterly wearing him out.

With an audacity that left Raelyn incredulous, Lil Son looked at his former friend from across the room and fixed his mouth to say, "You can't win in life, if you keep losing in your mind." His speculation was based on memories of a friendship that had long gone separate ways but somehow were stoked by the embers of unresolved pain.

He continued to jab at Raelyn with the piercing words, "At some point in life you gotta take a chance and start climbing the mountains in your life instead of always running the opposite way."

Immediately, Raelyn fired back, "How do you know the condition of my mind after almost ten years apart?" She broke into spontaneous laughter as she shook her head of golden tipped locks at Lil Son. "Well, you don't have to worry about my mind," she scoffed. "I'm getting the help I need and therefore I am winning." With strength gathering in her voice, Raelyn decided to fire her own shot as she explained, "It took me a long time to get to this place, but I finally realized that there was no room for me in your life along with your music and the enchanting spell of fame. Out of fear, I bowed out gracefully before I foolishly became the next casualty."

"But we never got to close out the music chapter within our relationship," Lil Son sheepishly replied.

"No," Raelyn responded, "we allowed our crazy love to get in the way of what our music ministry should have been."

Just then, Lil Son was struck with an epiphany that would have exploded his heart if he didn't share his feelings. "I want you to take this song that I wrote with one of the world's biggest Latin pop stars in mind. Then one day I started thinking about what it would feel like to have a love relationship again with the Creator, like the very first time I fell in love with Him. I scrapped my original idea for the song, started all over again, and instead wrote a love song to the One that made all my dreams come true.

"Raelyn, I want you to take this song, 'Loving You Again' and record it so you can tell the world about your love for the Creator. I realize you have walked away from the music industry because of all the dirty shenanigans that go on, but this could be the perfect vehicle to explain to your fans why you walked away from the fame and bright lights." He handed her a piece of paper scribbled with lyrics and waited anxiously for her reaction.

Raelyn could not believe that her years of struggle with anxiety and depression would bring her back in alignment with the person that became the bridge for her first big break in the music industry. She took about five minutes as she read the lyrics over and over, making sure the words would hold to the standard of her love affair with the God of the universe. Unable to find any fault with the lyrics, Raelyn finally looked at Lil Son and smiled..."I will do it."

Loving You Again
When I left and hurriedly walked away
Nothing in life compared the same
I thought life was over and somehow
I found myself at the end of the road.
My mind was made up and
there was no turning back to you.
Until a small voice cried within,
"Turn around and seek my face"
And now I will spend all of the rest
of my days loving you again.

Chorus:
Loving you is where I will begin
Loving you again in spite of my sin
Loving you again makes life worth living
This time I'm gonna live so I can live again.

As Lil Son started humming the bridge and hook, he noticed that Raelyn was staring at him. Knowing that his first love was looking into his face sent Lil Son over the moon. He wanted to believe that he saw the same twinkle in her eyes as when they were college students with crazy dreams about one day being famous and having their song played on the radio for the first time.

Raelyn reluctantly pulled her eyes away from the person she had once imagined would be her husband as she gathered the courage and determination to face the mountain in her life instead of running away. She slowly walked toward the window where Lil Son previously stood, briskly reflecting over the course of her life and her decision to walk away from the music industry. As she walked, the answer began to swell up on her insides as she slowly but emphatically began to feel that working with Lil Son would be a great way to stop running from her fears. Out of the corner of her eye, Raelyn caught her reflection in the window and noticed a slight strength of purpose building within. That was all she needed. She concluded in her mind that she would use this great opportunity to share with the world and her social media followers that the awesome Creator of the universe will never stop loving you in spite of your flaws. Raelyn quickly turned to Lil Son and collectively they said almost in unison, "Let's tell the world about His love."

CHAPTER 9
F. O. G. (Favor of God)

Dear Diary...

My friend and former college roommate is here. I'm so blessed to have her by my side. I just hope she doesn't see the fog that is hanging around my life.

God, when will my storm pass?

Although Belle had texted Sunshine before her morning five-mile jog, it took about two more hours before she finally figured out how to properly answer Belle's question.

Belle: Hi. How are you feeling today?

Me: I'm sure my storm will work itself out...eventually.

Belle: Everything always works out. Somehow life always seems to do just that.

And just like the unspoken privilege of best friends to enter a room without knocking, Belle burst into Sunshine's room at Queen's house later that same day after eating lunch alone at the mall. As the two girls sat on the bed exchanging small talk and trying to pass the time, Belle shared with her friend that she found it so much easier for them to talk in the dark back when they were roommates. "We would look out the window at the same distant sky completely oblivious of each other and it eerily felt like we didn't have bodies. Like we were just voices in the dark night sky," Belle concluded wistfully.

"Well," Sunshine snapped, "at least now you know how I feel all day every day. Just an empty shell for a body and a booming voice that cannot be heard by anyone."

"All I know," lamented Belle, "is that you shouldn't focus so much on the storm in your life that you forget the Creator of the storm and the universe."

"You do know that it's me that had to drop out of school to deal with this mental crisis?" Sunshine whined. "I'm the one that has suffered; I'm the one taking meds to hold on to the little piece of my mind that I have left."

Belle jumped up from the bed with her usual perky self and announced, "Roommate, I cannot wait to see how much more beautiful than before you will be after this storm passes."

"What, do you think I'm growing a new face?" Sunshine nervously implored.

"No, silly," Belle anxiously laughed, "the journey of going through a crisis melts us down to our essence or core self. This element of storm surfing or suffering transforms us and gives us a future testimony to share with others."

After a few more hours of banter and reflection, Belle finally announced, "Now let's eat." Sunday was a traditional day of feasting at the house of Mother Queen and Belle was determined not to miss any opportunity to eat the most disrespectful macaroni and cheese casserole on the planet.

The evening meal was a delight and the air remained filled with laughter and stories that only Queen could tell so eloquently. Anytime word hit the street that Queen was cooking, the house would fill with chatter and excited guests in high anticipation mode. Sunday dinner at Queen's was a weekly occurrence for friends, family and visiting clergy for many decades until recently when she started to slow down due to old age. Queen held her secret tight, but it was growing evident to anyone that got close for a period of time that she would grow tired often and needed to rest. Queen's heart was faltering and there was not much left to do other than have surgery. But, tonight Queen was delighted to host her usual friends and Sunshine's old roommate, who was in town for a visit.

As the sun was making its journey down the western sky, the core group of Sunday regulars had finally departed with satisfied stomachs and their to-go plates securely wrapped in aluminum foil. Sunshine relished the weekly dinner appointment with family, but the real treat was spending time alone with her grandmother once everyone left.

Sunshine waved goodbye to the last lingering guest and hurriedly blew kisses to her friend Belle as she entered her Uber for the ride back to her hotel room. Sunshine turned and walked briskly into the house. Taking a moment to thank God for such an amazing friend, she quickly closed the door and rushed toward the kitchen to help her grandmother with the few remaining dishes. Bending the corner in full anticipation of finally having some alone time with Queen, Sunshine quickly stopped dead in her tracks. Sitting at the kitchen table was one lone occupant remaining in the house that obviously did not get the memo regarding the fact that it was time to go...home.

"Ms. Pearl, I had no idea you were still here!" Sunshine wailed through clenched teeth. She reluctantly plopped down at the table, hoping she could outlast Ms. Pearl and her endless stories and blatant unconcern for not knowing when a party was truly over. As the first thirty minutes of her unscientific test slowly ebbed by, Sunshine finally worked up the nerve to glance over at Ms. Pearl. Her sole intent was to try and decipher whether the lovefest was coming to a close or headed toward an all-nighter with her grandmother. Sunshine followed the direction of Pearl's scowling eyes as they attempted to penetrate through her body, and finally concluded that it would be a very long night. What she didn't realize was how she was also about to be methodically tagged teamed by the church mothers in the makeshift surgical room.

Sensing that there was no escape, Sunshine buried herself deep into her chair and decided to allow the master class and whatever judgements to begin. With the slow and deliberate precision of a skilled surgeon, Ms. Pearl took a final bite of Queen's homemade German chocolate cake and let out a slow moan that would signify to any skilled cook that the recipient was on their way to heaven.

Pearl continued to keep her eyes closed for a tantalizing moment until it was awkwardly apparent that the last bite was completely gone from her palate. Opening her eyes from her magical journey, Pearl held her fork in the air as if she had just struck an imaginary bell to announce that her audience of one had failed to complete her homework assignment and it was time to dole out the punishment.

Clearing her throat to signal that class was in session, she stared intently at Sunshine and asked, "Baby, when was the last time you dreamed about your dream?"

"What dream?" Sunshine exclaimed, unaware of the left hook that was to follow.

"My point exactly," responded Pearl as she relished the moment to speak life into her best friend's grandbaby. "You have got to figure a way to stop killing your dream with your mind."

"Mother Pearl," Sunshine responded as she lowered her head, "I haven't been able to think about my dream since I was robbed of my mind on my college campus a little over a year ago. All I do now is struggle to make it in life and make it through another day."

"Don't say that," yelled Pearl as she grabbed the edge of the table in her attempt to stand up abruptly. "You, my child, have a good mind in you. Sunshine, you just gotta figure out how to use some of it."

"Yeah, the part that works," chimed in Queen.

Pearl rolled her eyes at her friend of over fifty years as she cautioned her to sit still and behave with just a wave of her church finger. Turning back to Sunshine, she pounced on the moment to awaken the giant within. "Baby, what are you going to do with all this pain that you have experienced?"

Sunshine remained silent and Ms. Pearl decided to dig a little deeper. She whispered softly toward the young girl as she gently caressed her teenage hand, "Sunshine, are you going to bury your painful college experience deep in the crevices of your heart hoping that the pain will magically go away? Let me provide you with a quick news alert: The pain ain't going nowhere without your determined effort. **Baby, you have to trust the process that He's not going to waste your pain.**"

Queen ignored all of Pearl's warning signs and glaring eyeballs as she suddenly decided it was time to insert herself into the conversation. She muttered, "Now this thing called pain is a little something I know about." Without looking at her best friend for approval, Queen announced in her booming voice, "This is my grandbaby!"

She reached around Ms. Pearl's wide body and positioned herself close enough to grab Sunshine's other sweaty hand. Queen continued, "Let me tell you what I know to be true...one of the things the experience of pain and sickness does is it strips away people that don't matter. When I went through my surgery, I lost almost all my friends. They just went to the wind, some with the parting words, 'If you ever need anything...just call me.' But let me tell you about the ones who stayed. Believe me when I tell you, I came to see them more precious than gold. My dear friend Pearl took the bus to my hospital bed every day for a week and gently combed my hair and smoothed lotion onto my face and hands." As a hushed silence filled the room, the two ladies hurriedly hugged each other and exchanged a fleeting glance that stood as a testament of their commitment to cover each other through all their storms of life.

Turning her gaze from Queen and back to Sunshine, Mother Pearl sighed. "I've cooled my heels for almost a year to give you this talk because I had to wait until you were ready to receive it." Looking her directly in the eyes, Ms. Pearl gave Sunshine her final marching orders. "Young lady, I believe you are ready to turn the storm of your life into the favor of God."

"But I'm scared. There's no map to tell me how to get back to the peace of my mind," Sunshine pleaded.

Mother Pearl gave Sunshine a big church hug and then abruptly released her grip so she could look her godchild directly in the face. Through her bittersweet first tears of the night, she whispered, "It is not by coincidence that it is very difficult to see clearly while in the midst of a storm. I've come to learn in my short eighty years on this planet that this is where God is going to do His best work. It is in the eye of the storm where the strong billows blow, and we cannot see our way that God will step in and determine our steps; the beauty of life is learning that you are solely responsible to determine the length of your stride."

The ladies prayed and poured into Sunshine until she was over-flowing with the strength of the greatest women of the Bible and filled with the tools necessary to move her life forward. Their impactful words had Sunshine walking on clouds as she headed out to meet up with Belle, fully confident that she must do all she could to get back to a place of mental restoration and peace. Not just home to the safety and comfort of her grandmother's house and the only home she knew other than her brief stay in the freshmen dormitory. The rallying cry became the determination to find a way to get home to the place in her mind that she had abandoned some time ago to the voices that invaded her thinking.

Without taking any opinion polls or surveys, Sunshine absolutely resolved in her heart that it was time to slay the negative thoughts roaming freely in her mind seeking to destroy her young life. She was determined to utilize the tools to obtain a fixed mind and commit to doing the hard work to return her mind to a place where peace, love and serenity could reside.

Heal me, O Lord, and I shall be healed; save me
and I shall be saved for thou art my praise.

Jeremiah 17:14

CHAPTER 10
Feels Like Home

*In three words I can sum up everything
I've learned about life:* **it goes on.**
Robert Frost

Dear Diary...

I'm ready to go home!

The Christmas season was in full swing across the nation and in spite of all the merriment in the air, Sunshine found herself breaking into sweat each time she thought about her decision to go home. Everywhere she looked, people were busy shopping and eagerly embracing the festive holiday spirit. *Christmas is supposed to be a joyous occasion*, thought Sunshine as she observed the shoppers darting from store to store all around her. But for Sunshine, the Christmas season only served as a constant reminder about her incident.

No matter what she did, Sunshine found it hard to shake the feelings of despair and abandonment that had attached themselves to the festive holiday season in her mind. The thoughts were tucked away deep inside her brain, immune to the wave of psychotropic medicine floating around in her bloodstream, looking to magically destroy any negative thoughts or feelings of melancholy.

"Not today, devil!" Sunshine spoke assertively, making a split-second decision not to hit the panic button and set off the sirens in her head in the middle of the parking lot. Usually, Sunshine found herself shouting at the top of her lungs, "Not today, devil," during moments of discouragement. It was not scientific in the least and no medical school in the land would vouch for its relevance, but Sunshine had become comfortable with how it felt flowing off her tongue. Those three words brought her comfort and made Sunshine secretly feel like she had a hand in her healing, along with the people in the white jackets and their endless supply of pills.

But on this particular Christmas Eve, the phrase "not today" held a different meaning. Today was the day that Sunshine was going back home to the psychiatric unit where she had spent several months of her life, to speak to the current patients and offer some cheer at the annual holiday party. As that moment quickly approached, all the memories of her breakdown came rushing into her consciousness.

The dark thoughts.

The voices.

The depression.

The pain of her journey from successful college student to the psych ward overwhelmed her mind, body and spirit. Unable to move past the sudden wave of emotion that swept over her entire being, Sunshine sat in her car with the seat belt tightly snugged across her body. She searched for the courage to open the car door and walk the enormous two hundred yards to the front door of the hospital and her destiny. She sat silently in her car, allowing all the fireworks of the last two years to flow through her as if the incident had happened just yesterday.

Slowly, Sunshine leaned back in her seat, closed her eyes, exhaled and hesitantly whispered the words of faith, "Just today, Jesus." Those powerful words had been lovingly placed in her spirit by Mother Pearl during one of their long talks. The phrase "just today, Jesus" had slowly become anchored in Sunshine's heart as she scaled the mountains in her life and found the undeniable strength to overcome. During the course of her illness, she realized that if she could just make it through each day with her Creator by her side, she would be alright. Sunshine uttered those words wherever she went, and it soon became the secret arsenal that she used to move mountains out of her way…one day at a time.

In that moment, paralyzed with fear as she wrestled with the monumental decision to get out of the car or not, Sunshine chose instead to continue sitting quietly. Her mind flooded with thoughts about her mountain-moving miracle of not hearing voices in half a year. And finally, Sunshine allowed a small smile to form on her face. Somehow, she was certain that this miracle was completely the work of her continued discipline of pill management and desire to be healed.

Miraculously, instead of the birds chirping all over her mind, Sunshine now packed that same space with the words of her hero, Nurse Hilda. Hilda often shared with Sunshine that, "Sometimes the fear won't go away. So, you will have to do it afraid. The secret power of courage is when you do it while you're afraid."

"Well, I guess I'm going to do this talk today scared to death," Sunshine finally mumbled out loud as she gripped the car door handle for the eleventh time that day. The two hundred yards to the hospital entrance seemed like the beginning steps of a lifetime as Sunshine slid out of her seatbelt and opened the car door. Moving to lean against the car, she nervously sucked in all the air possible and then exhaled, "I can do this." The significance of this day was monumental; the same hospital where she had been treated for her breakdown was now the site where today she was being led to her big breakthrough. By enduring the trials and pitfalls that were packed inside the eyes of her storms, it looked like she had weathered the journey and was now positioned to serve and give back. She had finally found the purpose of her suffering.

In a sudden moment of panic, Sunshine began to sweat profusely and the palms of her hands started to drip with moisture. Her thoughts flew back to a time when she had walked her college campus wearing gloves to mask her sweaty hands. Sunshine found herself attaching her thoughts to the familiar comfort of fear, questioning her worth yet again and considering whether she had anything of value left on her insides to say to the patients of the behavioral unit.

Sunshine suddenly saw her reflection in the rear-view mirror and said out loud, "Girl, how did you get out of your last storm?" She knew deep inside her belly that the odds were stacked against her coming out of the greatest storm of her life with a full recovery. But she had discovered that a "full recovery" back to her former self wasn't her ultimate goal anymore. Her life would always be different, but now she was different, too. Climbing her mountains had given her a strength of character she knew she'd not had before. Without her trial, how would she have found the strong woman she was becoming? With continued hard work, discipline, a renewed relationship with the Creator and a bold resolve to take her meds as prescribed, she knew she would continue to grow.

As she battled the conflicting desires to disregard her sweaty palms and the urge to rush back into the car and hope to disappear into the seat cushion, Sunshine decided instead to throw out another rhetorical question to herself. She whispered quietly, "If illness is God's way of getting people's attention, you could on some level conclude that what the world needs is more illness. If that's the way God operates, wouldn't it make sense that He would make everybody sick until the whole world finally wised up and did what He wanted?"

Unable to answer her own question, Sunshine finally gave herself a boost and started the train moving by declaring, "If you're going to go home, you might as well go inside." With that, the naysayers in her mind were overruled by a majority vote of one, and the conflict of returning "home" to the hospital was finally settled. Now the two hundred yards to the entrance were no longer so daunting. Fueled by her newfound internal strength, Sunshine courageously walked the steps necessary to make it to the hospital door and her appointment with destiny.

Standing at the nurse's station, Sunshine looked over the notes in her folder in preparation for the talk she would share with the audience. In a last-minute revision, she added "2X" to her paper as a reminder to repeat her mantra, "Just today Jesus," twice for effectiveness. Sunshine understood the power of words and felt it would be necessary to repeat her advice, "To believe in yourself and surround yourself with family and friends that will love you unconditionally," as the critical takeaway from her speech.

Sunshine continued to review her notes, although she knew she was prepared due to the direct result of the recent storm in her life that she had survived. This would be her very first motivational speech, and Sunshine was grateful for the text from Belle reminding her to "block out all other distractions before your big moment."

As she entered the room where she'd be sharing with the group, out of the corner of her eye Sunshine noticed a little girl sitting alone at the end of the room. The girl was foaming at the mouth, with a blank look on her face and an emptiness in her eyes. Cautiously, Sunshine walked toward the young girl, drawn by the allure of her dark sullen eyes. Impulsively, Sunshine reached out to touch the young girl and hold her hand. She noticed that her clothes were soiled and she was handcuffed to her chair. Immediately, a nurse raced over and admonished Sunshine to leave the little girl alone because "she hears voices and they will tell her to do harm to others." But Sunshine was unable to resist, and instinctively touched the little girl, anyhow. In that moment of defiance, Sunshine remembered the words of her mentor Hilda. "With your breakthrough, you can use your victory to help someone else just starting out on their journey."

In the spur of the moment, Sunshine decided to do something quite unconventional. She quietly closed her notebook, placed her jacket and purse on the table, and sat in the empty seat next to the girl. Every staff member in the room turned to look at Sunshine in amazement as she sat with the one patient who was always surrounded by vacant chairs. Several staff members conveyed their silent warnings with their rapidly blinking eyes as Sunshine decided that the chair next to this isolated individual was exactly where she wanted to sit.

"Don't sit there" was the collective muted cry. But, because everyone was in a state of shock that any person in their right mind would choose to sit so close to an unstable individual, not an actual word of caution was uttered. The silent bulging of their individual eyeballs was all they could muster, which Sunshine easily ignored.

While everyone strained their necks to get a better view, Sunshine simply introduced herself to the girl and asked the simple question, "What is your name?" Sunshine did not expect a response, but held out hope for a miracle as she looked into her eyes and saw the emptiness. The reflection staring back at her was just a blank face with eyes that focused on nothing in particular. The eyes just seemed to drift to a time and a place far beyond the short span of her years.

"My name is Sorrow," the young girl finally mumbled.

Sunshine scrambled to keep from falling out of her chair as she realized that the ostensibly silent girl had finally spoken. "What did you just say?" Sunshine inquired incredulously, hardly believing her ears. After a few minutes, the young disheveled-looking girl took her time to move her tongue out of the way for better clarity. This time, the girl repeated her words much slower, almost as if she knew that

Sunshine needed the extra help to comprehend all that was taking place around her.

"My name is S...O...R...R...O...W."

Instantly, Sunshine's mind once again flashed back to her mentor, Nurse Hilda, and her reassuring words that "you must determine in your heart to make it back to shore after your storm is over and absolutely bring with you the good news of your victory." With those words reverberating in her mind, Sunshine knew that she had to make the right decision in order to encourage others and continue her own journey toward healing.

Looking into the face of Sorrow, Sunshine saw her own journey reflected in her eyes and realized that in some sense, she was the same little scared girl that had arrived at the hospital some two years earlier. Squeezing Sorrow's hand for comfort, Sunshine quietly observed the name written on her name tag and smiled. She moved closer to whisper into the ear of her new friend, "Your name is Joy. You may not understand right now why you were born with the gift of mental illness, but you will survive your storm. You will one day share peace and love to all who come in contact with you. God is going to send some amazing people to help you through your storm."

Sunshine heard her name being called and hurried her way to the microphone. After thanking the medical staff for the invitation and briefly exchanging smiles with some familiar faces, Sunshine closed her eyes and exhaled. Moving her prepared notes to the side, she decided to speak from the heart.

"Christmas is a season of giving and receiving between loved ones and friends alike. I found myself in this hospital some time ago, and at the time I immediately resisted every opportunity of healing. I did not see any value in sitting around in my valley experience, and I absolutely struggled to get back to my original 'self.' It was only after I decided to take my prescribed medication and work within the treatment plan did I see things change regarding the 'new' me. I came to realize that my mental illness was the greatest gift that I could receive. Without that gift, I'm not sure I would have taken the time to understand my amazing need for the Creator of the universe to protect me on this journey through life." As Sunshine closed her speech, she looked over at Nurse Hilda and saw a broad smile covering her face. Shifting her eyes ever so slightly, she noticed that her favorite nurse was standing next to her new friend, Joy. Knowing that Joy would be in good hands, Sunshine ended her speech by once again reminding the audience how much she loved them and the medical team. As the tears of gratefulness started to pour out, she walked away from the podium, leaving her listeners with the summation of her journey through mental illness: "I thank God for my crazy."

Later, as she arrived back at her grandma's house from her trip, the magnitude of what she had faced over the last two years slowly started to flow and ebb through her body. Pulling into the driveway, she turned off the engine but remained sitting in the car in deep contemplation. As she let her experiences wash over her, she discovered a powerful truth. *When you stretch yourself, God will get in the flow.* She had certainly been stretched, and God had met her there. It had taken a lot of convincing to get Queen to agree to her traveling alone to Alabama, but Sunshine knew it had been worth it. She was beginning to understand now the importance of not always measuring herself by what was in her jar. Instead, she must emphatically trust what was in her jar and start pouring herself out into the lives of others. Sunshine smiled as peace washed over her. Her road to recovery would still be hard, she knew. But it would be worth it.

While sitting in the car lost in her thoughts, it began to rain. Although Sunshine was less than twenty steps away from her front door and could have easily made it without getting soaked, she was suddenly inspired to just get out and run and stomp in the rain.

Queen was in the kitchen preparing the evening meal when she peered out the window and saw Sunshine sitting in her car in the driveway. She let out a small cry of praise as she realized that God had answered her prayer to protect her baby and had brought her home safely from her trip.

Looking a little closer out the window, she noticed that it had started to rain and her grandbaby was back to what looked like foot stomping on the ground. With all her might, Queen yanked open the window and yelled, "Girl, get in this house! Are you crazy?" It wasn't strange for Queen to order Sunshine into the house because a storm was brewing on the horizon. Queen absolutely told everyone in her life what to do. As the oldest member of her tribe, it was generally assumed that Queen would get the last word in anything that she was involved in.

Not this time, though. Watching Sunshine dance, completely oblivious to her command, Queen saw a familiar glow on her face that she'd feared she'd never see again, as Sunshine danced and stomped her way around the yard. Queen quickly sat in the chair that was reserved for stirring her pots and keeping an eye on her neighborhood through her window. With Sunshine still outside in the rain, Queen realized that she was wrong for telling her grandbaby to run and hide and find shelter in the midst of every storm. *In my own life*, she reminisced, *I've come to realize that sometimes, you gotta just dance in the rain. Thankfully, Sunshine has realized that, too.*

During her dancing liberation, memories of the last several years came swooping over Sunshine; her life's bright outlook as she stood perched on the first days of her freshman year of college, facing a landscape of endless possibilities; seeing that sparrow on her windowsill, whose innocent chirping and building of a nest were really just the first deposits of her illness; how the epic meltdown in the cafeteria was a cry for help and the explosion of a ticking time bomb that had been ignored and unreported for far too long.

Sunshine inhaled a long gulp of air into her lungs. With the defiant confidence of a champion who remembered all the years of arduous work it took to win, she laughed as she shouted back toward her grandmother. **"Yes. I'm crazy!** I'm crazy if I don't take time to dance in the rain. I'm crazy if I don't continue to laugh through my storms and this journey called life." As Sunshine paused at the doorstep to take off her shoes and enter the house, she quietly whispered, "You could almost call me crazy if I never found the strength to teach the birds in my head to sing."

About the Author

Lyndon Pearson continues his journey in life in the small enclave of Vinings, Georgia just seven miles from downtown Atlanta. He practices inspiring others on a daily basis through his Life Coaching sessions and speaking engagements.

He is the author of two motivational books, **Are You My Father** and his current release, **The Birds In My Head Finally Learned To Sing.**

website: Lyndonpearson.com